TARA ELLIS

-Book One-

The Forgotten Origins Trilogy

ISBN: 1532804067
ISBN-13: 978-1532804069

INFECTED
(Formerly titled Bloodline)

To my family who graciously put up with my obsession over this story. Especially my daughter, Megan, for reading the manuscript and giving valuable critique. Most of all, my mom, Linda, for being there through every chapter to read, edit, and give encouragement.

The Forgotten Origins Trilogy

Infected

Heritage

Descent

Find them all at: www.amazon.com/author/taraellis

ONE

As I lie back in the tall grass and look up at the stars, I think about my dad. He used to bring me and my brother here, before he was killed. Dad was a cop in our small town in Washington State, nestled at the base of the Cascade Mountains. But his death didn't happen at work. That would have at least been understandable, or maybe even expected. Ironically, it was while my parents were on vacation. The authorities in Egypt said it was a simple mugging. Yeah right, nothing simple could have killed *my* dad.

Sighing, I turn towards my younger brother, Jake. His silhouette is visible a couple feet away. He was only eight when it happened, two years ago. I was old enough at fourteen to understand what was going on, but Jake was totally lost. Looking again at the stars, I try to escape into them, transported to distant galaxies the way I used to be when we came here countless times before.

Dad had really been into astronomy. He was always teaching me about the different constellations and stuff. Mom does her best to fill both roles, but it's an impossible task. A hand reaches out to grasp my right one, and I squeeze it reassuringly. My mom has a way of sensing my thoughts, and always knows what I'm feeling. She's situated in her favorite anti-gravity chair, tilted back all the way to allow a clear view of the skies.

Mom works at a nearby hospital as a nurse, and puts in some crazy hours. She's a strong woman, but the last two years have been difficult. She could have uprooted us and moved back to Nebraska so her parents could help, but she loves this town and didn't want to leave our friends and memories behind.

I'm glad we stayed because I'm so afraid of forgetting things. Like where Dad showed me how to hunt and camp. Or the trails in the woods near our house that Jake and I still use while talking about the outdoor survival he taught us. Places like this hill, where a large group of people from town are now gathered to watch the most anticipated galactic event of the decade.

A bright flash in the sky pulls me out of my thoughts. Excitement stirs in my stomach as I'm reminded of the reason we're here. Once every five thousand years a massive cloud of space dust and debris called the Holocene meteor shower passes through our solar system. The experts have predicted it will safely bounce off the atmosphere tonight, right above us in the Northern Hemisphere.

There's a ton of speculation over how dramatic it will

be. Dad was absolutely convinced it would be an historic event, almost to the point of being obsessed with it. Even two years after his death, I can feel the sense of urgency and importance he shared with me during our discussions.

Sometimes Mom and I like to watch the doomsday show on TV. You know, the one with all the crazy people hoarding food and ammo. We'll laugh about it and compare them lovingly to Dad. I've always wondered, in the back of my mind, if maybe he was right. I mean, my dad was a smart guy. Someone people listened to, especially about the important stuff. He never dug an underground bunker (that I'm aware of), but he was extremely preoccupied with being prepared for disasters.

All of a sudden, an especially bright meteor streaks overhead. A little bit of fear mingles with my excitement. What if? Sitting up, I pull my hand away from Mom's to rub at the standing hairs on the back of my neck. In the faint moonlight, I can see that there are several dozen people on the hill with us. I'm surprised there aren't more, given all the media hype over the past few weeks. I had even heard there's a bunch of nuts hiding out nearby in the mountains, convinced aliens are going to invade. Apparently, they want to be the first to go. Laughing quietly, I shake it off. Everything will be okay.

"Alex?" I can hear the concern in Mom's voice, further convincing me that she can seriously read my thoughts.

"I'm fine, just stretching a little." Cracking my knuckles for emphasis, I smile in the darkness, knowing that she's cringing. Mom hates it when I do that, something about it being un-ladylike.

"Need a blanket?" Holding one out to me, she is obviously not convinced that I'm okay. For as long as I can remember, whether I'm running a fever, nursing a scraped knee or a broken heart, Mom thinks a blanket will make it better. I don't know, maybe she's right. I take the blanket.

"Thanks, it's getting a little chilly. How about you, Jake? You need one too?" Turning my attention to my little brother, I pick up the tradition of blanket therapy.

"Thanks, Alex," he says in his sweet, quiet voice. I spread the furry comforter over both of us. "Do you think he's up there?" The question hangs in the air for a moment, neither Mom nor I able to answer. "I hope he gets to watch. Dad wanted to see it so bad."

"I'm sure he is," I finally choke out. "No doubt he's got the best seat in the house." As if to confirm my statement, a brilliant meteor erupts from one end of the horizon to the other, briefly lighting our faces. Several whoops call out from the crowd. I know the big grin on my face probably looks silly, but I really don't care.

Seated near us in their lawn chairs are Mr. and Mrs. Jones. They run the local grocery and butcher shop, a total cliché of the whole "ma and pop" thing, but they totally pull it off. There isn't anyone in our town of around four thousand who doesn't know them. I've been buying candy from them my whole life, and they are very dear to me.

"This is already the best meteor show I can

remember in my seventy-five years on this planet!" Mr. Jones says to his wife and everyone else nearby. I lean forward so I can make out their faces in the shadows.

"It's supposed to be the brightest we've had in thousands of years," I explain. "The Egyptians described it as the gods descending from the heavens."

Mrs. Jones reaches back and gently pats my arm. "Oh!" she gasps, turning around as another, even bigger meteor arrives. We all point while the crowd starts laughing and clapping. For this unique moment, we are all kids again, each experiencing something amazing for the first time.

Another rock is hot on its literal tail; this one with a blue and green glow to it. Something new. Sparks erupt from it and fall towards us as it passes over. I wonder if any of those pieces are reaching the ground. Probably not. I know it's rare for meteors to turn into meteorites, because most of them burn up in the atmosphere long before getting anywhere near the surface. I have seen something vaguely similar to this before, but the fluttering in my stomach grows as I grasp that this many, so fast, really is historic. "You were right, Dad," I say quietly to myself.

Before long, almost all of us are on our feet, unable to contain our excitement. Children start running around the clearing, yelling and screaming at each other like they're watching the best fireworks display ever.

The sky is now lit up with dozens of smaller meteors falling all at once, larger ones coming a bit closer every few minutes. The cheering starts to die down as the adults begin to sense things quickly going from fun to unknown, or perhaps even dangerous.

"Alexis?" Mom only uses this form of my name when it's something important. I know she is looking for reassurance, but I don't think I can give it to her, because this is starting to freak me out too! "Maybe we should go home now," she says, hesitant.

"I think we're just as safe here as we would be at home," I say, not wanting to miss a thing, no matter how scared I get. Besides, it's true. "If one *does* happen to hit the ground, the house wouldn't stop it anyway." I realize a little late that I am *not* encouraging Mom with that approach. She grabs onto my arm, clinging to me like she's going to fall over.

"We need to go *now*. Jacob!" she yells, while releasing me and starting to collapse her chair. Peering over her shoulder, she watches for incoming meteorites, as if she'll have to dodge one at any second. I can't say I blame her. My little brother is quick to obey, and huddles close to Mom. His eyes are so wide with fear that I can see the falling stars reflected back at me.

The meteor shower continues to intensify, and the "oohs" and "ahhs" from the crowd are now mixed with cries of alarm. Some spectators start running to the parking lot, located at the bottom of a short trail. During normal times, this is a nice park, but tonight it's closer to something out of a sci-fi movie.

I decide to give in and gather up the warm blanket, its comforting powers not strong enough for the current situation. Maybe Dad should have built that bunker after all. Smiling at this thought in spite of my growing fear, I help Mrs. Jones pick up her chair. "I can carry it for you," I tell her, as we all start for the trail.

We're almost there and I'm beginning to think we've escaped the apocalypse, when a sudden explosion from above rocks us, knocking Mrs. Jones to the ground! Screaming, I drop the chair and cover my head with my arms, kneeling down beside her. Jacob crashes into me, also yelling, and Mom throws her arms around us both, using her body to protect us.

A roar unlike anything I have ever heard fills the air. We all look up and see a huge ball of blue flame scorching the sky. It's hard to tell how close it actually is, but it's certainly inside our atmosphere. In fact, I think it's only a few hundred feet up, and so bright that it hurts my eyes. Squinting, I watch it move west, towards the mountains.

Another explosion rips through the night and I recognize them now as sonic booms. I've read somewhere that those can happen with large meteorites. This one is definitely making it to the ground. Smaller chunks of rock are breaking off and showering the night with various colors before burning out, as the main body rapidly moves away. I'll have to come back during the day and see if I can find any of those pieces. That is, if we make it through the night.

A final sonic boom reaches us from the distance, not nearly as loud as the first two. I can still see the meteorite, though not as bright, and as the light goes out I hear what has to be the sound of an impact.

"Maybe the crazies were right!" I say to the stunned

group around me, since it did in fact land in the Cascades. Apparently, my attempt at humor is not appreciated, and I am met with glares instead of laughs. "Seriously though guys," I press on, "it was just a meteorite. NASA even said there could be some near misses. I think it was obviously a bit closer than everyone predicted, but I'm sure it'll be okay," I explain, waving my hand over our heads. "Look, it's even starting to slow down."

I must be more persuasive this time, because Mom lets us out of her awkward embrace. Resisting the urge to rub away the dents her fingers made in my skin, I stand and wrap the blanket around my shoulders instead.

"Are you okay, Mrs. Jones?" Mom moves over to the older woman's side as Mr. Jones helps her slowly to her feet. Her nursing instincts have taken over, and I suppose that is a good distraction. The five of us move cautiously down the trail now, leaving a few brave souls still standing in the grass behind us.

By the time we reach the parking lot, it's obvious that the worst is over, and there's less panic among the people still here. There's even some nervous laughter from a group of our neighbors standing next to their cars. Looking up, I only count a dozen meteors, and they aren't as impressive as the ones just five minutes ago.

Waving at a friend who's driving away, relief floods me. That simple act brings back a feeling of normalcy that before now, I didn't know meant so much. I guess I was as terrified as everyone else.

"Thank you so much for your help, Katie," Mr. Jones says to Mom as he helps his wife into their sedan.

Mom gives him a brief hug and says something to him that I can't quite hear. He chuckles, and gives us a final salute as he settles himself into the driver's seat.

My mind is racing as we head to our full-sized truck on the other side of the parking lot. Were there more meteorite strikes in other places? How widespread was it? Did they cause damage or even kill people in other towns? Is this it, or was this a prelude to a bigger event the government isn't telling us about? I plan on attacking my computer for answers as soon as we get home.

I don't know why, but seeing our truck makes me happy. Like I thought it was going to disappear or become a part of this new, twisted reality up on the hill. There it is though, just as we left it, completely unchanged by the bizarre events around it. We toss the chair in the bed of the truck, but I take the comforter with me to the front seat.

"Wanna drive?" Mom asks. She's standing in the open door across from where I'm now huddled. I'm always begging her to let me drive, especially since I got my license when I turned sixteen a couple of weeks ago.

Actually, to not be asking her all the way back here was totally out of character for me. So when I shake my head no, she frowns. The lines deepen in her forehead, and I can tell she's concerned. While I'm sure this whole thing scared her, she probably still expects me to simply be excited about it. Especially since I was doing my best to convince her everything was okay only a few short minutes ago. Not wanting her to call me on my bluff, I toss the blanket aside and suck it up.

9

"Of course I want to drive! You really believed me?" Putting on what I hope appears to be a real smile, I slide across the bench seat and snatch the keys from her hand. The dim light must help, because she smiles back at me and walks around the front of the truck, her step a little lighter.

Jacob climbs into the backseat, reaching over to seize the blanket. "I'm cold," he complains, "and hungry."

"Well, it's too late to get anything in town, but there's a frozen pizza and rocky road ice cream at home!" Mom offers, her spirits lifted by the suggestion. We all agree that greasy cheese and chocolate are exactly what we need.

As we pull out of the lot, Mom erupts into a series of violent sneezes. It startles me, especially since she doesn't have allergies. After four or five of them, it seems to have passed and she laughs at herself, sniffing.

"Bless you! Geez, what was that?" I ask, studying her. The street lamps illuminate her face randomly as I drive under them, and a sense of foreboding fills me. For whatever reason, the sneezing bothers me more than the crazy scene we just drove away from.

"I must be getting a cold," she says, while digging around in the glove box. Coming up with an old tissue, she blows her nose fiercely. "I'll be fine, silly. It's just the sniffles."

Just the sniffles, I tell myself. Looking to my left, I can still make out the dark, looming mountains. Somewhere out there, not too far away, is what's left of that meteorite, still hot from its journey through space. A shiver runs up my spine and I find myself envious of my brother wrapped up in the blanket behind me.

TWO

Opening my eyes to an intense light, I roll over in bed and the warmth on my shoulders confirms my suspicions. Sunlight! Smiling, I remember that it's Saturday. Even though it's early April, here in the Pacific Northwest, sunshine can never be taken for granted. We live in what's considered the eastern part of Washington State, but since we are located on the slopes of the Cascades, we often get caught in a rain shadow. Summers are usually nice and hot but spring is unpredictable.

Sitting up, I rub at my eyes and try to focus on the window. Yup, that's definitely sunshine! Throwing back the covers, I decide to spend the day outdoors. Maybe I'll even take Jacob fishing at a nearby creek. Sometimes it has rainbow trout this time of year.

Glancing at the computer on my desk, my joy wavers slightly. I'm drawn over to it, turning it on with a hesitant hand. I had eagerly looked for news stories when we got home last night and to my relief, there hadn't been any mass reports of casualties or anything like that. From what I could find, most of the northern states and Canada got the show of their lives, or millennium really. There were local reports of numerous meteorites entering the atmosphere and several that were suspected to have made impact. One gal in our county claimed a piece landed in her pool, but that was under investigation.

The one that we saw seemed to be the biggest, and the scientists were saying on the late news that they were organizing a team to go look for it this weekend. It could have been as big as five feet when it hit, which is huge for a meteorite. However, it landed in an extremely rough, secluded area, so odds are that it might never be found.

I don't know why I'm afraid to look at the stories this morning. I just feel ... off. Like there is something hanging over my head and if I acknowledge it, it's going to fall. Stupid, right? I bring up the news sites and browse through the top stories, most of which are about the Holocene shower. It's everything I expect to read and nothing weird. Several on-line pictures confirm that it was as crazy as I remember. It hadn't been a dream. So what's bothering me so much?

Shrugging, I exit out and turn off the computer. Maybe it's because of Dad. Thinking back, I try to recall what he had said about the shower. I know he studied it extensively because it was a rare event, but I don't know why he thought it was *so* important.

Three years ago, he talked about taking the whole family to Egypt to see his parents. I was always bugging him to go, but when he suggested it for my birthday and that we watch the shower to celebrate my "Sweet Sixteen," I was surprised. I didn't think we could even see the meteors that good from Egypt. I know I asked him about it, and what was it he had said? Something like: "it didn't matter and we'd be safer." I thought his response was strange and out of character for him. He said something else another time and I drum my forehead, trying to remember.

Closing my eyes in concentration, to my surprise I am taken back a year later, to the day my parents left for their trip to Egypt. The last time I ever saw him. We were in his office and he was getting their passports. He hugged me and whispered that we might have to change my birthday plans. I had pulled back and looked at him quizzically. My birthday was still almost two years away. Smiling, he drew me in for one final squeeze. He told me not to worry, that we would talk about it when he got back from Egypt. Only he never returned. With everything that happened in the weeks after, that had seemed so irrelevant that I'd forgotten about it. I still don't see why it should matter now.

When my birthday had rolled around, there was no way that Mom could afford to take us all to Egypt. I don't know if she would have, even if money weren't an issue. There were too many bad memories. She gave me a list of options, but in the end, I decided that I didn't want to be anywhere else but here. I had a modest party with my family, a few friends from school, and my best friend Missy flew in from Idaho. We grew up here together, but her family moved last year because her dad got laid off and Idaho was the only place he could find a job. It sucked.

Grabbing a robe off my bed, I wander down the hall and stop at the door to Dad's office. I go in every once in a while, when I'm feeling alone. The door squeaks slightly as I push it open and step inside. I love the smell of this room, a mix of polished wood, old books and antiques.

Flipping on the light, I look around at all the familiar, comforting things that belonged to him. Hanging on a peg next to his desk is his duty belt from work. His Glock pistol, Taser, and other items he'd purchased himself are still there. It hasn't been touched since he worked his last shift, four days before he died.

I walk across the room to my favorite item, nestled in a rack on the far wall. Running my hand down the smooth stock of an aged rifle, I let it linger on the intricate carving on the wooden butt. I assume the work was done by my great grandfather, who had passed the rifle down to his son, and then to my dad. Who knows? Maybe it dated back even more generations than that.

The rifle may be old, but it still works. Dad taught me how to hunt with it. I shot my first deer not far from here, hidden in a blind that he built himself years before.

There are two other guns on the wall, both which look just as nice, but this one is my favorite. The memories associated with it are precious, and although it was never formally left to me, I think of it as mine. Mom didn't say a word the first time I took it out by myself, about a year after his death. I didn't bring anything back. I'd had a nice little buck lined up in my sites, but after several heartbeats ... let it walk away. It just hadn't seemed right.

Shaking my head to clear my thoughts, I turn to the other wall, where there's an assortment of fishing poles. Grabbing two of them, I turn to go, but am stopped short when I see a book out on Dad's desk.

Leaning over, I try to read the tiny text on the yellowed, brittle paper, but I can't figure out what it is. Setting the poles against the wooden desk, I sit down to examine it. The cover is made of worn leather, and even though I have poured through his collection several times over, it doesn't look familiar to me. Frowning, I try to read the title, but it's too faded and I don't even think it's in English. What is that, Latin?

Turning the pages back to where it was left open, I can see that there's a combination of what I'm guessing is Latin and hieroglyphics. Hand-written notes are scribbled all over the margins in what has to be my father's unique script. "Since when did Dad speak Latin?" I ask the empty room. "And who left this here?" Perplexed, I rise to go find Mom and question her about it.

Before I reach the hallway, I hear wet, rattling coughing from her room next door. Dropping the book back on the desk, I rush towards the sound of my mom gasping for breath.

"Mom! Are you okay?" She's sitting in the middle of her bed, surrounded by used Kleenex. Her nose is red and her eyes have heavy bags under them.

"I'm okay now," she says as she tosses another wad of tissue onto the pile. "I just needed to clear my throat. I swear I feel like I'm drowning in snot!" Lying back against a stack of pillows, she looks closely at me. "You're not sick. That's good. Going fishing?"

I look at the poles in my hand. I don't even remember picking them back up. "Oh! I was thinking of taking Jacob down to the creek, but we don't have to go. It wouldn't be right leaving you here when you're feeling this crummy."

"Don't be so dramatic, Alex. It's only a head cold. If it'll make you feel better, you can get me some breakfast, and bring me a bunch of vitamin C. Then go do whatever you want, there's no reason for the two of you to be cooped up in here with me." Rubbing at her nose again, I can tell she is trying her best not to cough.

I know Mom well enough to understand it's best to do whatever she says. I would never win this argument, and she'll be happy if Jacob and I enjoy the sunshine, even if she can't. "Got it!" I tell her, smiling. "I'll be right back with your order."

I go to the kitchen, but just stand staring into the open refrigerator, unsure of what I want to attempt. None of us are great cooks. That was Dad's department. There's a carton of eggs and a couple of other things I could use, but honestly, the only reason we have eggs is because our neighbor keeps bringing them to us. She's very proud of her hens.

After some internal debate, I close the door without removing them. Instead, I grab a pack of frozen waffles.

Sticking four of them in the toaster, I go in search of some vitamins. I locate them in the back of a cupboard at the same time that the waffles pop up.

I'm rather proud of myself when I place the food and other items in front of my mother. I even found some orange juice. "Thank you, Alexandria," she says with a mock British accent, tucking a napkin regally into her nightshirt. Laughing at her, I'm glad that she still has a sense of humor. That's a good sign.

"Jacob! Breakfast is ready!" I yell on my way back to the kitchen. I find him already there, his mouth crammed full of food, including what was going to be mine. Fighting the words that threaten to come out, I instead get the box back out of the freezer. It's easy enough to make some more. Jacob can be a bit ... sensitive, and I want today to be positive. "How about we go fishing when you're done?"

Looking at me with a huge grin on his face, he nods excitedly. "Seriously?"

"Seriously," I reply, pointing to the rods in the corner for proof. "I think we might find some trout down in the creek."

"Sweet! I haven't even gotten to use my new pole yet. Grandpa has to stop getting me that stuff for Christmas; I have to wait too long! Watch him get me a snow sled this summer for my birthday." Jacob rolls his eyes for emphasis as he swirls the last of his waffle in a puddle of syrup.

Eager to leave, he drops his empty plate in the sink and runs to his room. Our golden retriever, Baxter, chases after him. The two have been inseparable ever since an old friend of Dad's gave him to us, right after his death. It was strange at the time, because we didn't even know him, but Mom was polite about it and didn't want to refuse the gift.

Once the guy left town, she swore that we'd have to find the dog a home. It was the day after Dad's funeral and Jacob hadn't spoken or interacted with anyone for almost two weeks. It all changed that afternoon when Baxter went to him in his room and proceeded to lick Jake's face until he started to giggle. It was like music to my mom's ears. From that moment on, boy and dog were one, and Mom was in love. Baxter seemed to know Jacob needed his help, and it was amazing to see how therapeutic their relationship was. It took time, but Jake slowly came back to us and Baxter stayed.

Running back down the hall to my room, I pluck my phone off its charger and send a quick message to Missy. While waiting for a response, I decide to look through some pictures I've taken and slide my finger over the screen. I love this phone! It was my main birthday gift, and even though I had begged for several months, I never really thought I would get it. Dad always had a thing against cell phones. He and Mom eventually had to have them for their jobs, but they weren't smart phones. I feel kinda guilty, because mine is nicer than Mom's. I thought I might get an old style like hers, but I didn't expect this.

A little chirping noise indicates I've got a response and I quickly read it: *Ya, sunny here 2. Going on a bike ride. Wish U were here!!!!!!* ☺

Missy likes to use lots of exclamation marks and smiley faces. I already miss her. It was nice to see her for my birthday, but it seems like months ago, not two weeks.

We've probably been setting some sort of texting record ever since, although both our parents laid down the law about not texting after ten at night and turning them off if we're driving. I guess the thrill of it is wearing off a little bit, because I didn't even take it with me last night. It dawns on me that I could have used it to record video of the meteors, and groan at the missed opportunity. It probably would have gone viral!

I type out a quick response, telling her that Jacob and I are going fishing, and then toss it on my bed. No way am I taking it out in the woods with me! I know we'll end up in the water, and I would die if it got ruined. Not to mention it was made very clear to me that it would NOT be replaced if something happens to it.

By the time I get ready, check in on Mom and go out to the garage, Jacob and Baxter are there waiting for me. Jacob has some lures in his hand and seeing me, holds them up. "How about these?"

Smiling, I open up a different tackle box. "Those are nice ones, but way too big for these trout." I pull out some foul-smelling glittery fish paste and red salmon eggs. "These will work better." Putting them back, I latch up the small box and pick it up. "You wanna carry the poles?" In reply, he drops the hooks and grabs them from me.

"Should we bring some sandwiches?" he asks, always thinking about food like any ten-year-old boy should. I consider his question and the time. It's almost nine, and we've got a good half hour hike each way plus we like to take our time. Figure at least two hours in the creek and we're definitely going to be getting hungry.

"Hold on," I tell him, and disappear back inside. A short time later, we're on our way with a backpack full of water, sandwiches, and power bars.

The trail from our backyard is small but well worn and we follow it silently. The sun is filtered through the trees, creating patterns across our arms and backs, warming the morning air enough to remove the chill. The heat has reached the ground today and the smell of warm pine needles surrounds us. I love days like this and never get tired of the scenery. It's timeless here in the woods, and always alive with animal sounds and whispers of wind in the trees.

I pause, tilting my head. That sounded like more than wind. Jacob and Baxter quickly disappear ahead of me, around the next bend.

We have just left the mix of green leafy trees that line the edge of the forest: mostly cottonwood, birch, and maple. I am now in the middle of massive pines and cedars, the lowest branches above my head. I step off the path and onto the bed of needles, looking back to where I think I heard the voices. The thick leaves of the birch and cottonwood obscure my view behind us, but I'm not hearing anything now. Perhaps it *was* the wind. Turning to go, I step back onto the tramped down dirt created by years of use.

"*Alexandria.....*"

I spin back around, certain I heard someone. "Who's there?" I demand, scanning the trees again. Nothing.

"Alex! Hurry up!" This time the voice is ahead of me, and undeniably belongs to Jacob. Baxter comes bounding towards me, and I kneel down to pat his head.

"Hey, buddy." Taking a hold of his furry face, I look him in the eyes. "Is there anyone out there? Do you hear anything?" Cocking his head to one side, he gives me a quizzical look. Pulling away from my grasp, he stares intently at the thick foliage down the trail, even sniffing the air. Chuffing, he turns his deep brown eyes back to mine and licks me on the nose. His decision final, he runs back the way he came and I get up to follow him.

Baxter is a smart dog. If he doesn't feel threatened, then I shouldn't either. "Coming, Jacob!" Trotting to catch up, I resist the urge to look back again. There is nothing there except my imagination. Today *is* going to be a good day.

THREE

Once at the creek with our feet in the water and poles loaded with stinky fish bait, I feel better. We call it a creek because half the year it isn't very big, but the other half it's more like a river. The melting snow and rain from the mountains above feed into it, so it's always icy cold.

Our favorite fishing hole is an amazing place that's also our best-kept secret. We've never encountered anyone else here and it's as if it were made especially for us. Created by thousands of years of running water, the carved-out rocks make a bowl about twenty feet wide and up to ten feet deep. It's fed by a small waterfall and has just enough logs caught up in it to make the fish feel safe. Along one side, moss covered stones provide the perfect place to sit. On days like this, the sun warms them when it's directly overhead.

We've been at it for over an hour already without

any bites and are debating if we should try digging for some fresh worms. I decide to stay put while Jacob starts scraping at the dirt with a rock. Baxter catches on quickly and aggressively digs his own hole nearby.

"I called Brent while you were getting ready," Jacob informs me, while holding out a small worm. Taking it from him, I put it on his hook and hand the rod back.

"Oh. So why isn't he fishing with us?" Brent is Jacob's best friend. They've been hanging out pretty much every day for over a year now, since he moved to our neighborhood. I assume he called to invite him fishing. Both of his parents work on the weekends, so he can usually come over. Better than being home alone.

"He's sick. So are his parents."

"Well that's too bad." I look over at him when the silence draws out, like he's expecting me to say something more. I find him staring at me. "What?"

"They were all there last night." Again, he looks at me with his dark Egyptian eyes, like that's supposed to mean something.

"At the park? I didn't see them. They must have gotten there after we did." A small butterfly floats through the air between us, and I'm momentarily distracted by the bright colors of it wings. Refocusing on Jacob, I can see that he really seems concerned about something. "So what? Are you upset Brent didn't find you?"

Clearly frustrated with me, he shakes his head. "They were *all* there last night, Alex. Them, Mom, and Scott. Brent said that he's sick too. Don't you think that's *weird?*" Scott was another friend from school that he hangs out with.

"Okay, so they all got the same cold. That happens. You and I were there last night and we're fine. Oh! You got something!" His line has gone tight, pulling the rod down towards the water. Reacting on instinct, Jacob yanks it straight up, setting the hook. With a few turns of the spool, he pulls a trout close to two pounds from the clear water.

Laughing, I quickly scoop up some water in our big bucket that we always bring. Jacob expertly frees the fish from the hook and drops it in. Dad taught us the trick of keeping them alive until we get home. They taste better that way, or at least, *we* think so.

"So worms it is! Get to work Baxter, we need more." Baxter barks back at me excitedly and then resumes digging in the hole he had been creating.

Jacob smiles, seeming to relax again. "I guess you're right, Alex. I dunno, maybe it's because I don't like it when Mom's sick."

Pulling him to me, I give him a quick hug over the fish bucket. I understand his fear. Looking into his eyes, I ruffle his thick, dark hair the way I used to when he was smaller. "She'll be fine, Jacob. We'll take good care of her. Tonight she eats trout!"

After breaking out our sandwiches, we spend another two hours fishing before calling it quits. By the time we head home, we have three nice-sized fish. I plan on cooking two of them and sticking the third one in the freezer. I'll give it to Mr. Jones the next time we go to the store.

The trip back is uneventful and I turn on the gas barbecue to pre-heat before heading inside. I find Mom sound asleep and figure it's best to let her rest. On my way back out I grab a good filet knife, some tin foil, butter and a lemon. I may not be much of a chef, but I know how to cook a fish.

Jacob has taken care of the unpleasant business of killing them, so I agree to do the rest. By the time I have them wrapped up in foil and cooking, it's well past three. It'll be an early dinner, but that's okay. I'm already hungry and if I am, then I know for sure Jacob will be.

Within a few minutes, the smell has my mouth watering and I realize we'll need something else to go with it. Heading back inside, I search through the canned veggies and come up with creamed corn. Some frozen Texas toast should round it all out nicely. After heating it all up, I go back out to get the fish. It doesn't take long to cook.

I think about it for a minute and then decide to set the table. Mom has really been emphasizing this lately. Several nights out of the week she doesn't get home until late, so Jacob and I have gotten into the habit of eating in front of the big television in the family room. On nights that she is home though, she makes a point of setting the nice kitchen nook that takes up a corner of our large country style kitchen. I don't know if she'll be up to eating with us, but I know it would make her happy.

On my way down the hall to get Jacob, I look in on her again. She's still asleep and I can see her chest rise and fall in a nice, steady rhythm. It's pretty stuffy in her room, but I'm afraid that if I open the window she might get too much of a draft. She looks comfortable enough, so I'll leave her alone.

After stuffing ourselves, we put the dishes in the sink for later and Jacob disappears outside with Baxter. Mom's still snoring away so I go back to my room and catch up with Missy on our day.

According to her, biking is for dorks and she would have much rather been fishing. Her younger sister still has training wheels on her bike, so she spent the whole time going in circles waiting for her to catch up. I laugh at how she describes it all. I'm able to picture exactly how she would look when saying it. Missy has always made me laugh. She has a way of knowing just what to say. I tell her about our big catch and my gourmet meal, wishing I had my best friend there to share it with. After several more exclamation marks and smileys, we say goodbye.

Her dad has promised to get a new laptop this next week and we're both looking forward to being able to video chat. Her old one has had a broken camera for months now. Looking at my own computer, I decide to check out what's new before crashing in front of the TV.

It would appear that nothing fell into that one woman's pool, at least certainly not a meteorite. The scientists are still trying to locate the crash site, based on radar and satellite images, but they don't sound too optimistic. Tired of the news, I switch over to my social media account.

I'm not exactly what you would call a social butterfly, but since I've grown up in this town, I do know a lot of people. I'm a junior this year and play on the school soccer team and write for the high school paper, so my inner circle of friends tend to stem from those two groups. Although my friend list is a little over two hundred, I only talk regularly with or follow around twenty. Even so, the amount of them posting about how sick they are is alarming. My apprehension grows when I figure out that most of them were in the park last night. I actually count the status updates... ten. I remember seeing at least seven of them there. It suddenly gets a little harder to breathe.

I take a deep breath and sit back in my chair. Stupid. I'm being stupid. We're all friends and go to the same school. We ride the bus and eat lunch together. It would make sense that several of us would come down with the same cold. But it was literally within hours of each other. A few said they were sick before going to bed and the rest had it when they woke up this morning. This was just strange. Frustrated at my own conflicting thoughts, I shut my computer down.

It's not even six yet, but I still want to put on my comfy pajamas. I'm thinking it's going to be a popcorn and movie kinda night. Grabbing a big blanket off the foot of my bed, I decide to give in to it and go all out.

I stop again at Mom's door and see that she's sitting up, the fading light of the day reaching her on the bed. "Hey Mom, how are you feeling?"

"Like I've been hit by a truck. A very big truck."

Searching around on the bed for a moment, she comes up with a remote and turns on the TV. A horrible coughing fit grabs hold of her and I cringe at the sound. I can't remember ever seeing her this way before. "Alex," she says, finally able to catch her breath. "Would you please close the blinds for me? That light is killing my eyes."

Crossing the room silently, I do as she asks and then sit down next to her. "Are you all right? Want me to call someone?"

Smiling, she takes my hand and shakes her head. "No, it's just the flu. I've seen this so many times at work, but I guess I've never had it full blown before. I'll be miserable for a while, but I've always been healthy so I think I'll be okay. I promise to let you know if I need a doctor. Thanks for entertaining your brother. I'm sure he had a good time fishing. "

Feeling a bit reassured, I try to smile back at her and then remember that I saved her some dinner. "We managed to catch a few trout today! I put some in the fridge for you. I can heat it up."

Wrinkling up her nose at the thought, she shakes her head. "I can't really stomach the idea of eating much more than crackers right now. Can you get some for me, and maybe a soda and more Advil?"

I manage to find everything requested and even locate another box of tissue and some cold medicine. I reposition the pile of pillows behind her and turn on a small nightstand lamp instead of the brighter overhead one.

"I'd give you a kiss right now, but you seriously don't

want this," she says, taking a swallow of medicine. "In fact, you should go wash your hands. That's the best way to avoid getting it."

"Get what Mom?" We both turn to look at Jacob standing in the doorway with Baxter.

"Oh it's only a flu bug, Jacob. It isn't anything to worry about. I'll be back to normal before you know it! Now come give me a quick hug before I go back to sleep."

He crosses the room hesitantly, as if he's afraid she's lying. Once he gets close enough to see her better in the dim light, he seems more convinced and jumps onto the bed, throwing his arms around her. "Please get better," he begs, his voice muffled in her blonde hair. Looking at me over the top of his head, the love and concern for him in her eyes is obvious.

Patting him, she then gently pulls his arms from around her neck. "Of course I'll get better. I love you, bug." Shooing him off the bed, she swats him on the behind. "Now go wash your hands so you don't get sick too."

Satisfied for the moment, he smiles and dodges beyond her reach. I realize then that Baxter is absent, which is odd, because he never misses an opportunity to snuggle on a bed. Looking back I see that he is still in the doorway, quivering. I give him a questioning look and he whines at me in response. Before I can call him, Jacob is running through the doorway and Baxter quickly follows.

Not seeming to notice the exchange, Mom tells me goodnight and reminds me again to go wash my hands.

After making sure I can't get her anything else, I follow her instructions.

Back in the family room, I find Jacob and Baxter already on the couch. They're all wrapped up in the blanket that I dropped earlier while getting mom's stuff. Jacob is busy trying to find a movie to watch, so I plop down next to Baxter, planning to finish our conversation. He looks at me boldly, in a way that only an intelligent dog will.

"What was that all about, buddy?" I ask quietly, stroking his head. Looking intently at me for a moment, he then leans forward and softly touches his nose against my forehead. Folding his paws in my lap, he places his head on top of them and sighs. It wasn't like I expected him to answer me, but for some reason that I can't explain, I believe he just did. I don't know what he's trying to tell me, but that feeling of danger I had last night is suddenly back with a vengeance. As darkness starts to press in against the windows, the three of us huddle together under the blanket.

FOUR

Sunday morning isn't starting out so hot. It took forever to get to sleep last night, even though Jacob and I stayed up late watching stupid movies. It was good to laugh. We started that tradition during the horrible weeks after Dad died, when Mom stayed in her room for a day or two at a time, in a deep depression. Fortunately, her parents flew out and helped get her and us through it. Come to think of it, I believe Grandpa Fisher was the first one to use the stupid movie treatment. There wasn't much laughing back then, but it was a good distraction that grew into a new family time.

I wish my Grandparents weren't in Nebraska. It's way too far to drive very often and they couldn't afford to fly back more than once, maybe twice a year. They were just here for my birthday, so we probably won't see them again for several months.

My restless sleep last night was filled with odd

dreams about running through the woods, trying to get away from whispered words that I couldn't understand. Twice I woke up to check on Mom. I think that she was coughing and that's what drew my attention, but when I tiptoed to her room, she was sleeping quietly.

Then there was Baxter. Normally, he isn't a problem and goes through the night nestled up to Jacob. Last night though, he woke me up around three. There he was, just sitting there staring at me. Scared the heck outta me. He was right next to the bed, his snout resting on the mattress beside my pillow. He whimpered at me when he saw that I had opened my eyes. I was too scared at first to move and by the time my brain caught up with my heart, I realized it was just him.

Thinking he needed to go outside, I took him to the back sliding door in the family room, but he just looked at me like I was stupid. Making that sound only a dog is capable of (you know the one where they are clearly done with you), he padded in to Jacob's room and didn't come back out the rest of the night.

Now, for some reason I have woken up again and it's not even eight. It's Sunday! I don't usually get up until Mom makes me. Lying here, I can tell that it's useless to try and get back to sleep and it's still too early to text Missy. She would kill me for waking her up.

I grab a book off my nightstand and flip through the pages. I haven't even started it, and I can't quite seem to read more than two sentences at a time. This reminds me of the old book on Dad's desk yesterday. I had almost forgotten about it. Deciding to give in and get up, I throw on some sweats and head for his office.

I find the book right where I left it and pick it up on the way to Mom's room. I don't know what I expected, but I'm shocked when she looks up at me. The shades are still drawn, but enough light is bleeding in around the edges to reveal the deep smudges surrounding her eyes. The red on her nose has spread around her mouth, which looks raw and sore. I don't think I've ever seen her shiny blond hair in such a matted mess. She's always been thin, but fit and strong. Now, she seems frail and weak.

"Mom! You're worse." Going to her, I put a hand to her forehead, finding it dry but very hot. Her neck actually *looks* swollen and I realize it's her glands.

"Yeah, this is the worst I've ever felt," she confirms. Her voice is coarse, like someone who smokes three packs a day. It's seems an effort to even talk.

"I should call Dr. Wells." He has been our family doctor for as long as I can remember, and I'm confident he'd know what to do, because I sure don't.

"No, don't bother him. My cough is actually better, which was the most concerning thing. So long as my lungs are clear, I should be fine. My headache is a little better too; it's just this God-awful aching, sore throat and glands. I'd swear I have the mumps if I didn't already have them as a kid."

Looking closely at her, I'm trying to decide if she's being honest with me. It's true that she hasn't coughed yet, and her breathing isn't raspy like yesterday. "Okay, but if you still aren't getting better by tonight, I'm calling. Deal?"

"Deal," she agrees. "I see you found the book." Taking it from me, she flips through the pages. "I got this out Friday night. I meant to give it to you yesterday."

"Why?" I'm transfixed by the fluttering paper, like something's going to spring out from them. "What is it?"

"I don't know." Looking at me, she seems to be debating something. Her hands becoming still, and she holds it back out to me. "It's from your father."

"Dad?" Confusion engulfs me, along with several questions, as I take it back. "I don't understand."

Sighing, Mom tucks several loose strands of hair behind her ear. "Alex, the day of the ... mugging, when your father was shot, he didn't die right away. You know that I was there with him. Well, after a short fight with the man who attacked me, he shot Adam in the chest. It all happened so fast, I don't even remember the guy running away or me screaming for help." Pausing, she takes several breaths and I think she must be fighting back tears. But looking at her, I realize that while it's obviously hard to talk about, she's totally composed. She's just winded from talking.

Coldness starts to spread from my stomach, as I comprehend that she doesn't seem upset at all. I've never heard exactly what happened. It's mainly due to the fact that normally, Mom can't even discuss Dad without getting choked up. Grandpa Fisher held me that night of the phone call (they were staying here with Jacob and me), telling me he'd been shot and killed while protecting Mom from a robber. But that was all. This is the first time that Mom has ever given me any details of that horrible day.

Looking at me now, her deep blue eyes are glazed with fever, but clear of any strong emotion. I hold the book to my chest, a small shield between us.

"I held his head in my lap as he told me he loved all of us. He knew he was going to die, Alex, but still he took the time to tell me that the book was in his bag and I was to give it to you the day after the Holocene meteor shower. He whispered something else, but I couldn't hear him and then he was gone. I've kept it ever since. I have no idea what it is, but it must have been important to him." Pulling the covers up around her neck, she lies back in bed, seemingly exhausted by the conversation.

Staring at her, I look...no, *search* for any hint of the pain that I know has to be there. Is she sicker than I realize? Closing her eyes against my questioning gaze, she turns her back to me. "Would you get me a pad of paper and pen please? I don't need a doctor, but I do need you to get me some stuff from the store."

Stunned at the abrupt end to what should be a meaningful exchange, I stand up and back away from the bed, the book still clutched to me tightly. "Sure Mom, I'll be right back. Um, thank you for the book and for telling me what happened." Her back still to me, she remains silent. I realize there are tears running down my cheeks and I wipe at them absently. I open my mouth, wanting to say more, needing something, but not knowing what.

The silence drags on, and it's clear that she is done talking to me. Drying my face, I turn and leave the room, telling myself that it's because she's sick. That's all it is.

When she's feeling better, she'll hold me in her lap and we'll have a good, healthy cry together. Maybe we'll talk more about that day and why he wanted me to have this book. She'll tell me it's okay and that she's here for me, like she always is. Right now though, I am feeling very alone.

A cold nose nudges my hand, and I realize I am sitting at the kitchen table, silently sobbing. Baxter is at my side, like he always is when I'm upset. Looking down, I discover that I've gotten tears on the leather bound book, the dark stains spreading slowly. This makes me cry even harder and I slip off the chair and onto the floor, burying my face in Baxter's thick coat.

I'm not one to cry much or to wallow in self-pity, so I'm embarrassed at my outburst and thankful for my silent, patient friend. It doesn't last long and as soon as I sit back and start wiping at my nose, Baxter is quick to assist in licking up my tears. Smiling, I bat away his tongue and push him down so I can rub his tummy. He loves that.

"Who's a good dog?" I ask him, scratching his sweet spot and making his leg kick. "Who's the best dog in the whole world?" Writhing in delight, he smiles a doggy smile, knowing that he, in fact, is the best dog in the whole world.

Taking a deep breath, I know I have to suck it up. Now is not the time for any breakdowns, even mini ones. I have to take care of Mom and Jacob, and I can never let Jacob see me cry like that. It would put him in a panic and I don't think I can deal with anything else right now.

I find a pad and paper and take it in to Mom. She is still wrapped up in the blanket, watching some nature show on TV. "Thanks, Alex." Taking them from me, she writes out a list and then hands it back. "My wallet should be by the door. I think there's some cash in there, or else Mr. Jones should be okay letting you use my bank card."

"All right, I'll be right back." Turning to go, I just can't leave things this way. "I love you, Mom."

"I love you too, hon." It was nice to hear her say it, but it falls flat and her attention never wandered from the television. I quickly leave the room.

Writing out a note to say where I went, I drop it on the counter for Jacob in case he wakes up. "Stay here Baxter, I'll be right back." He looks at me, disappointed, but stays like I tell him to.

Grabbing the truck keys and Mom's wallet, I head out to the garage. Pausing in the doorway, I change my mind and go back inside. For a reason I don't understand, I take the book from the kitchen table and go back to my room. Standing there, I look around until deciding on my closet. I hide it in the very back, under an old stuffed bear. Feeling strangely better, I leave for the store.

FIVE

Standing in the health and medicine aisle, I study what is left on the shelves. Not much. Several people share the narrow space with me, most of them coughing and looking almost as miserable as Mom. Grabbing the last bag of cough drops, I drop it in my small basket where a few things are already piling up.

Looking again at the list, I snatch up the next-to-last bottle of Advil and then head to the paper products. Time to stock up on tissue.

I can't believe how many people are in the small store, and it seems that almost all of them are sick. Most of them look like Mom did on Saturday morning. I have to admit, that in spite of my reassurance to Jacob yesterday, this is really starting to creep me out.

Cramming three big boxes of Kleenex in with the other items, I fail to notice anyone walking up behind me, and jump when I hear my name.

"Alex Mubarak, right?"

Spinning around, I find a guy I know from school

standing behind me. I haven't talked to him much lately though, since he's a year ahead of me. "Yeah, I'm Alex. You're Chris?" He appears to be studying me, looking carefully first at the things in my basket and then back at my face. His dark eyes are intelligent and troubled.

Nodding, he points at the stuff I'm buying. "You sick? You don't look too bad." It dawns on me that I'm still in the sweats I put on when I got up this morning. My long dark hair is pulled back loosely in a scrunchie. I blush slightly. I don't normally wear much make-up even on a good day, and this is definitely *not* a good day. My eyes are probably still red from my cry session, completing my image of total chaos.

"Umm, no. My mom is though. I'm getting this for her. You're okay, too?"

Holding up a pack of toilet paper, Chris grins. "Totally healthy, just getting some essentials." Trying not to blush more, I can't help but smile. He smiles back, his bright teeth stark against his darker complexion. The angular lines of his face give away his Native-American heritage and I remember that his dad is full Okanagan Indian, his mom half. The thought takes me back to the first time we met, at a youth group three years ago. Some of us were talking about our heritage and when I explained I got my unusually bright brown eyes due to being half Egyptian, Chris started calling me tiger eyes. Ironically, it was the same nickname my Grandpa Fisher had for me since I was a small child, but for him it was because of the gemstone, not the animal.

After Dad died, Mom turned away from the church.

He had always been the one with the desire to seek out God and it seemed like his dying gave Mom all the proof she needed that he wasn't a caring God. I didn't have the heart to argue with her, and so hadn't been back. I had good memories of my time in the teen group, even though I had only gone a few times.

"How's your mom doing?" I ask him, avoiding comment on the toilet paper.

His demeanor changes drastically and he frowns at the ground. "I don't know, haven't seen her in a few weeks." When I raise my eyebrows questioningly, he shrugs. "She left and hasn't come back."

Not knowing what to say to that, I search for something intelligent to comment on, but draw a blank. "Oh," I mumble. Well, that'll impress him.

"Don't you have a little brother? Is he sick too?"

Glad for the change of subject, I quickly jump on it. "Jacob is his name, and no, he's fine. He told me yesterday though that his best friend and another boy from school are sick. I think their parents are, too. My mom says it's the flu but it sure is spreading really fast."

We start to walk towards the front of the store, where there's a line at the register. Most of them are sniffing and hacking. I feel like I should have a mask on. In fact, I notice someone else in line is actually wearing one. Smart.

"I walked through town to get here," Chris explains, looking down at me with that serious expression again. "Not many are people out. I think most of them are either in bed, hiding, or coming here for cold and flu stuff. I saw a few ambulances go by in the short time it took me to get here. I think almost a third of the congregation at church was gone this morning and the rest are in various stages of this. It's all really strange."

Wanting to ask him more about his mom, but not knowing how, I just nod in agreement. I hate to think of him on his own. His dad left them when Chris was really young; he had been very open in sharing that at group. It was just him and his mom now. They don't have any other family nearby. I realize he's almost an adult but it still seems wrong. At least he'll be graduating in a couple of months and so I guess then it won't matter.

We haven't had any classes together this year and he's with more of the football crowd while I'm in the keep-to-myself crowd. He's said hi to me in the hallway at school a few times, but otherwise this is the most we've said to each other in two years. I am beginning to wish I had at least brushed my teeth and put on some jeans before running out the door.

"Wait a minute," I say to him, his last comment finally sinking in. "Did you say that a *third* of the people at church were gone and almost everyone else was sick? How's that even possible?"

"I really don't know. I've never heard of anything like this before. I mean, not this many people so *fast*, plus it's almost summer. We don't even usually get the flu around here this time of year."

The lady standing in line ahead of us turns around, holding a tissue to her nose. "My neighbor was taken to the hospital by ambulance this morning," she tells us, her voice muffled. "I heard that several people have even died. The CDC is coming here to investigate. It was on the news this morning. They're calling it some sort of super flu." Turning back around to move forward, she begins to cough violently. Everyone takes a few steps back from her and she finally regains her breath, but has to hold onto a display rack for balance.

Chris and I look at each other, the fear of everyone near us tangible. I feel a sudden sense of urgency to get back home and check on Mom, feeling guilty now for judging her. She's sick, and needs my help.

The line inches forward and I grab some crossword puzzle books off the shelf as we pass by. Mom loves to do these even though she's never finished one. It'll be a good distraction for her.

"Alex, if your mom is okay tonight, you should come to our youth group. I don't know if we're going to have it with everyone sick. I'll have to call around and see how many can make it, but it's usually at the church at seven. Here's my cell number, text me." Taking one of the Kleenex boxes from my basket, he writes his number on the side.

Not sure how to respond, I mutter okay and take the box back from him. It might be kind of nice to get back into something positive like that, but I'm not sure how Mom would react. She's been so opposed to anything churchy. Maybe I'll just go and not make an issue out of it.

It's finally my turn at the check-out counter and I find Mr. Jones's daughter there, her nose red and eyes puffy.

In all the years I've been coming into the store, it's never changed. One big, long counter spans the front where the meat is located and the only register sits. While other stores in town have been updated, this one remains timeless. Either Mr. or Mrs. Jones have always been behind the counter. Always. My feeling of unease increases as yet one more "wrong" piles up with the others.

"Is your dad sick, too?" I ask his daughter, Mrs. Stamos. She is married to the mayor and used to teach at the elementary school when I was little. I always liked her and I hate to see her so sick and upset.

"Very," she answers quickly. "Mom is in the hospital. I'm waiting for someone to get here so I can go be with them." Taking a deep breath, she tells me the total and then finally recognizes me. "Oh … Alex. I'm sorry, hon. This has been a very crazy day. How is your family?"

Handing over the cash, I take the two bags from her. "Jacob and I are fine but Mom is in bed. I think she might be getting better though, or at least her cough is. I hope your parents are all right. Let me know if I can help." Smiling weakly and nodding she turns her attention from me and on to Chris.

Dismissed, I back away feeling a bit lost. I head for the exit but Chris catches up to me as we step outside. "So text me, okay? It'd be nice to have you back," he says, turning to walk down Main Street.

"Sure, I'll see how things are when I get home.

Maybe I'll see you tonight." Waving goodbye to each other, I feel reassured that there is someone else I can talk to that seems unaffected by the flu.

When I get back home, I find Jacob in the kitchen eating cheerios. "Your phone's been ringing," he tells me in between bites.

Running back to my room, I finally find the phone under my pillow and check the history. I missed three calls from Missy. Maybe I should have texted her earlier after all. Calling her back right away, I flop down on my unmade bed. She answers before the second ring. "Alex! Why didn't you answer? I was so worried!"

Smiling at her exaggerated concern, I assure her that I'm alive and well. "Why are you so freaked out? Did you hear about the flu here?"

"Hear about it! It's all over the news, Alex. They're calling it a super bug and it's spreading fast. They even said that it started in Washington State and is already in Oregon and Idaho."

Normally, I'm someone that wants to know everything, but I'm really wishing I could block it all out. "Yeah, I just got back from the store and heard that the Center for Disease Control is coming to town and a bunch of people are in the hospital. I ran into this guy from school there and I swear it seemed like we were the only two that weren't sick."

"What guy?" Missy has a way of zeroing in on the important stuff.

We talk for over half an hour and I finally tell her I have to go after Mom starts calling for me. I promise to call or text later and let her know how things are going. Just before we hang up, I hear her sneeze.

SIX

Jacob and I eat fish for the second day in a row. I guess it was a good thing that I forgot to take it with me this morning to the store. I feel almost guilty eating it, but I promise myself to go fishing again next weekend. I'll take Mr. Jones twice as much, when they're feeling better.

Today was a weird day. Mom wasn't looking any better and I felt really bad that I made her wait for me. She took the cold medicine, the Advil, and more vitamins. I made her eat some soup and then she went back to sleep.

I had to call the hospital for her, to let them know she wouldn't be in to work today or tomorrow, at the minimum. I didn't recognize the person I spoke with, but she didn't sound sick. Apparently, they have had almost half of the staff call in due to themselves or family members being ill. The hospital is on over-flow protocol. She explained that meant they are out of beds, so they have to set up tents in the parking lot. There are several smaller towns that the hospital serves since it's the only one in the area. When I asked her how bad it was, she said to tell my mom to get well and that they need her back as soon as possible.

I haven't had a chance yet to talk with Mom about it. She's been asleep the whole afternoon. I know sick people are supposed to sleep so I haven't bothered her, but I keep checking on her to make sure she's breathing okay. The wet rattle from Saturday night is gone now so I take that as a good sign.

Even though it's been another nice, sunny day, my brother and I haven't ventured any further than our backyard. After watching the news, I think we're kinda scared to go anywhere.

The top story out of Seattle is what they're calling "The Spring Flu Epidemic." They showed men and women in white hazmat suits right smack dab in the middle of our little town of Omak. They estimate that based on reports from local hospitals, we appear to be ground zero.

They compared this outbreak to the Spanish Flu of 1918, except that the infection rate for our current bug might end up being even worse. They say that so far it's around thirty percent of the exposed population, but that secondary exposures are just now showing up at the doctors so it may climb. Mom was right, it's definitely a virus, but they haven't isolated the strain yet. Even though it's obvious that they don't know what it is, they are still urging everyone to go get a flu vaccine. The government is doing everything it can to ensure enough vaccines are available. Whatever.

The virus is all over Washington State, and has shown up in Oregon, and Idaho. It's expected to be seen in other neighboring States by tomorrow. I called Mom's parents, Grandma and Grandpa Fisher. They don't watch much television, and hadn't heard anything about it yet in Nebraska. Probably best, or else they would have been really worried. I assured them that Mom was getting better and everyone else was healthy.

I debated trying to find the number to Egypt to call Grandma Mubarak. I have only met her three times in my life and haven't spoken to her since she called once after Dad's death, and another time to tell Mom that Grandpa Mubarak had died. It was last summer, and they had been planning on coming to visit us. I'm pretty sure that it was only Grandpa who wanted to come. He actually called the week before to talk with me, to make sure I was going to be here during the whole visit. I was a bit surprised, because I had always gotten the impression that us kids weren't of much interest to them. I know that Grandpa shared the same desire for studying the past like Dad did, so maybe he wanted to talk with me about that, or go through Dad's books.

Whatever the reason, I'll never know. He had a massive heart attack the weekend before the trip and never made it out of the hospital. Grandma Mubarak cancelled the trip, obviously, and then never rescheduled. She was not comfortable making such a long trip on her own, and we are the only family here in the States. Dad was their only child. I finally decide that if she is concerned, she will call us.

I push the last of my dinner around on the plate, my thoughts taking away my appetite. Baxter whimpers at me, seeing an opportunity and I give in, scraping the fish into his dog bowl.

"Done, Jacob?" I turn my attention to my little brother, who seems as lost in his thoughts as I was in mine.

"I'm not very hungry," he admits, shoving the plate away. "No one answered the phone at Brent's house." He looks at me with his dark eyes as if it's my fault, like I should be doing something about it.

"I'm sorry Jacob, I know you're worried. Why don't you call again tomorrow and if there's still no answer, we can go over together."

"Promise?"

"I promise," I assure him. "Here, help me with the dishes." Handing him my empty plate, I start unloading the clean ones out of the dishwasher.

As we work silently, I realize that we haven't gotten one of those automated messages from the school, telling us that it's been cancelled. It's surprising since such a big deal is being made about this epidemic, but in a way I'm glad. It'll help to have that routine to follow and for there to be something normal and familiar to go to.

As I put the last of the dirty plates in to wash, Jacob scurries into the adjoining family room. "Want to play with me?" he asks, grabbing the video game controllers.

Although killing aliens sounds like fun, I've been

waiting all day to get some time alone to look through Dad's book. "I'm going to read for a little while, but I'll come out and play with you after that, okay?"

Shrugging, he flops on the couch next to Baxter, who had given up on more scraps. By the time I walk to my room, he's already lost on a Martian planet.

Even though I know it's silly, I have a sense of relief when I find the book right where I left it. Lying on my bed, I turn on the lamp next to it to push back the gathering shadows. Realizing how late it's getting, I dig the piece of cardboard torn off the Kleenex box from out of my pocket.

Staring at Chris's number for a while, I think about the text I want to send. I finally decide to keep it simple: *This is Alex. Sorry, Mom still sick and I need to stay home. Maybe next week?* I send it before I can change my mind ten more times. To my surprise, he answers almost immediately.

That's okay, it was cancelled anyway. Too many sick. Next week for sure. See you tomorrow.

It was weird to read a text that wasn't full of smileys and exclamations. Thinking of Missy, I send her a message too, asking how she is, and then turn my attention to the book.

About the size of a small paperback, it is obviously very old but I can't find any date on it. In fact, I don't understand anything on it except for what my dad wrote, which was a lot. Every other page has words or glyphs underlined or circled. The only one I recognize from some of his other books is the clear image of a vulture.

Off to the sides he wrote what I am assuming were comments in regards to what was marked.

Going to my computer, I pull up a good search engine and try to find a Latin translator dictionary. The cover is too worn to read, but the first page has what I figure is the title: Antiqua Aegyptiacis Historias. It seems obvious that historias means history, and antiqua possibly antique. I quickly find what I'm looking for and within a couple of minutes have an answer: Ancient Egyptian History. Makes sense. My dad's bookshelves were full of history books, a lot of them about his native Egypt.

Grandpa Mubarak was extremely proud of their heritage, according to Dad. I guess it was a bit of a scandal when he married Mom instead of following his family's tradition of returning to Egypt after college to find a suitable Egyptian wife. Instead, he married his first love, got a job in Seattle, and never moved back to Egypt. Grandma and Grandpa Mubarak had been living in Washington State because of Grandpa's engineering job. They stayed for several more years after the wedding, but went home to Egypt after I was born.

Then Dad left his job as a history teacher at the University in the city, for one at our local High School. He never explained the change to me, other than wanting to raise his family in a better setting, closer to nature. It wasn't until I was ten that he became a policeman. I think it had something to do with a midlife crisis, or a shrinking economy and teaching jobs. Maybe both.

Whatever the reasons, he never lost his interest in history so I'm not surprised at this particular book.

Except for that it's in Latin. Of course, he may have been drawn to its age and that he would have to translate it, much as I am doing now. That would be just like him.

What I don't understand is the way he gave it to me. Why in the world would this little book be so important that it was the last thing he ever said? How come it had to be *after* the meteor shower? It was crazy, and thinking about it is giving me a headache.

Looking again at his notes, it's all random dates, historical names, Egyptian locations and hieroglyphs that mean absolutely nothing to me. Most of it is in pen and in places, it's bled into the fibers of the parchment to the point that I can't even read it. Totally frustrated, I set it aside and decide to sleep on it. I feel like I'm missing something obvious, but have no clue as to what it is.

I close out the search engine and pull up some news sites. The "Spring Flu Epidemic" is still the leading story, and is now rapidly marching across the nation in record time. I don't want to read about it.

Looking at my favorite conspiracy message board, I see that several posters already have theories on government-planned viral genocide, secret lab experiments gone wrong and numerous other similar headlines. I don't have the heart to open any of the threads.

I decide I need to check in with some of my school friends. I find that a few who posted yesterday that they were sick, haven't said anything new today. I send some messages to them, asking how they are and then look up my Aunt Tammy, Mom's sister.

They live in Nebraska too, and we haven't seen them since Dad's funeral. There isn't anything current on her page, so I send her a message also, updating her on us in case Grandma didn't tell her. It's too bad none of my Grandparents have taken advantage of social networking.

Just as I post a silly comment on Missy's page, my phone alerts me to a new text. It's from her: *My whole family very sick, sis in hospital!!!! GTG, ☹ ☹ ttyl!!!!*

My heart sinks as I read it. Missy might complain a lot about her sister, but I know how much she loves her. Wishing I could be there for her, I simply text her back that I love her.

Deciding that kicking some alien butt does indeed seem like a good idea, I turn off the computer. As I pass by my bed, I stop and stare at the large comforter in a heap on top of it. Longing for the time that I took my mom's concern for granted, I gather it up in my arms and go find my little brother.

SEVEN

I'm in the forest again, alone on the trail and running through the twilight, as branches claw at my face. I can hear the whispering. It's all around me and I can't get away from it. Tripping over a root, I fall onto a bed of pine needles, but the ground gives way beneath me and I drop down into darkness. Opening my mouth to scream, no sound comes out, and all I can hear is the air whistling past me as I fall, the smell of damp rotting earth engulfing me.

Right when I think I must be close to the bottom, there is a rustling of feathers and a vulture flies by. As it turns back to look at me, I realize we are both now moving forward in a shadowy, grey world. It goes ahead of me and I somehow follow, soaring through a dim, twisting tunnel.

As a source of light begins to glow far ahead, I become aware of stone walls rushing past on either side.

Reaching out, I touch the cold rock and as I do, dark text begins to seep to the surface, moving beyond me before I'm able to read what it says. While I'm straining to see it, a word written in lighter paint floats away from the wall. It evaporates as I fly through it, like it's made of smoke. Confused, more images leap out at me as the passage brightens.

Looking ahead towards the opening, the vulture is silhouetted in the light, hovering. Opening its beak, it says my name: *"Alexandria …"*

"Daddy!" I'm sitting in bed, a pillow clutched to my chest. Sweat clings to my forehead and causes my nightshirt to stick to my back.

The vulture had spoken in my dad's voice. He was trying to get my attention, to show me something. I know this with a conviction that doesn't make sense, but nothing has made much sense lately.

Mt heart hammering, I close my eyes and take several slow, deep breaths. I don't usually remember my dreams, so I go over what I saw, trying to hang on to those tendrils of imagery before they fade away. The forest, the whispers, falling into the tunnel. Words on the walls, a vulture with Dad's voice leading me to the entrance. *Dark* words were on the wall, and *lighter* ones were floating at me. The vulture. Opening my eyes, I jump from the bed. I understand!

Turning to the nightstand, the glowing numbers on my clock tell me it's almost six and the alarm is about to go off. Pushing down the button to silence it before it can start, I pick up the book next to it and hurry over to my desk. I turn on the lamp and wipe the sleep from my eyes; I don't have much time before I have to get ready for school.

Opening the delicate pages, I confirm what I already know; on the first page of text about half way down is the vulture hieroglyph. I've seen this a lot in the books Dad has. He'd circled it in pen and then written in the margin beside it. Everything else he wrote on that page was in dark ink, *except* for the word *Alexandria,* which is written in pencil.

Startled, I read everything in the notation that includes my name. It was a description of a location in *Alexandria,* Egypt. It's one of the largest cities in Egypt now: My namesake.

Grabbing a pad of paper and pen, I write out my name. With confidence growing, I flip through several more pages, looking for anything written in pencil. I find it ten pages in, on the bottom margin. The only word in pencil is *follow.* I write it down. Half way through the book, I almost miss *the* crammed in between several sentences about pyramids.

There are less than a hundred and fifty pages to the whole book, so it isn't long before I find the next one. Only, it isn't a word. It's the vulture hieroglyph, clearly drawn in pencil on the inner margin, near the spine.

As I carefully draw the picture, the correlation between this cryptic message and my dream becomes obvious. *Alexandria follow the vulture.*

I drop the pen and lean back from the desk, rubbing at my temples. How is this even possible? Did my subconscious pick up on it and cause the dream? Impossible. I hadn't even looked at half those pages, so I couldn't have possibly known what it was saying.

Not expecting to find any more text, I go back to the book and thumb quickly through the remaining pages. To my surprise, there is one more on the very last page. {*Hollow*}. Well, that didn't help any. What in the world was that supposed to mean?

Alexandria follow the vulture { *hollow* }

My breath catches in my throat and a sob escapes me. My father is trying to speak to me from the grave and I can't even understand what he's saying!

There's a loud pounding on my door and I jump, startled. "Alex!" Jacob yells, knocking again. "Are you up?"

Looking at the clock, I see that it's already past 6:30. How long was I sitting here, staring at those simple words? "Yes Jacob, I'll be out in a minute." His footsteps retreat down the hallway and I push back from the desk.

No shower for *me* today. Ripping the paper I wrote on from my notebook, I carefully fold it. I pull on my favorite jeans and then stuff the paper in my back pocket. Taking the book into the closet, I set it under the watchful bear after grabbing a shirt off a hanger.

I finish dressing and run a brush through my thick, wavy hair that falls a few inches past my shoulders. Looking in the mirror, I scrutinize my face. Missy has forever claimed to be envious of my dark lashes, saying that it looks like I always have mascara and eyeliner on. Applying some shaded lip gloss, I decide it's good enough and pick my phone up off the floor, where it was charging.

Although it's early and I know Missy is sick, I can't wait. I have to message her. *Missy U have to call me as soon as U can. Must talk!!!!*

Slowing as I pass Mom's room, I peek in and see that she appears to still be sleeping. Rushing into the kitchen, I quickly heat up a couple of waffles and pour a glass of juice. Taking it back to her bedroom, I try to carefully place it on her nightstand without waking her. However, as I'm backing away, she rolls over and looks at me.

Expecting her usual smile or some other form of acknowledgement, I'm thrown off by her silence. She's just staring at me, like a scientist studying a bug.

"I...um, got you some breakfast." Nothing. I awkwardly shift from foot to foot. "Jake and I have to leave for school." Reaching out, she picks up the orange juice and takes a long swallow. "Mom, are you okay?"

Pausing with the glass still up to her mouth, I can tell that she realizes how odd she's behaving. Slowly lowering it, she blinks rapidly several times and finally smiles at me, cocking her head slightly to the side. "I'm actually feeling much better Alex, thank you."

I wish she'd stop smiling at me. It's making me very uncomfortable for some reason. Looking for something to focus on other than her, I see the crossword puzzles I left by the TV yesterday. Grabbing them, I hold them up so she can see them. "I got these for you, maybe you'll feel up to it today?"

Nodding, she takes them from me and finds a pen among the cold medicine and Kleenex. Opening one, she begins studying the clues. It's like I'm no longer in the room.

"Well, I have to go. I've got my phone if you need anything." Without looking up, she waves me off.

Turning around to leave, I see that Jacob is standing behind me. He has a cross look on his face as he stares at Mom. When she continues to work the puzzle, he walks away and I follow.

We both pick up our backpacks that are hanging on hooks in the kitchen, by the garage door. I take an old-looking banana off the counter before leaving, thinking I might get hungry before lunch.

"Did you feed Baxter?" I ask Jacob as we get into the truck.

"Yeah, I put him in the backyard. What's wrong with Mom?"

I've always appreciated his ability to get to the point. You know just where you stand with him. "I don't know, Jacob. I think it's because she's still sick. Sometimes that can make you act weird."

"It's kinda how she was after Dad died." I meet his gaze and wonder at how he can be so smart.

"You're right. It is sort of similar, but I don't think it's the same thing. Before, she was depressed." Turning my attention back to the road, I navigate a turn. "Right now, her body is getting over something really nasty so it's going to take a while before she's back to her old self again. It'll be okay." Hoping I sound sure of myself, I try to hide my real emotions from my face. It dawns on me that I didn't even consider telling her about what I found in the book, or share my dream. I don't know why.

I briefly think about sharing it with Jacob, but decide that since it's confusing and upsetting for *me*, it would be even worse for him. Right now, he has enough to deal with. It wouldn't be fair for me to dump that on him, too.

Hopefully, Missy will call me back soon and I can run it past her. She's pretty silly, but very smart. While I work to maintain my 3.4 GPA, Missy has always had a 4.0, even with advanced classes. Perhaps she'll be able to point out something obvious that I can't see. Sometimes it takes someone outside a situation to see it for what it really is.

As we approach the elementary school, Jake turns to me, arms folded across his chest. "I don't understand *why* we have to go to school if this whole flu thing is so bad.

Won't it make it worse to have us all together?"

Once again, his common sense can't be argued with. "I don't know, Jacob. You and I obviously aren't going to get it, or else we'd already be sick. Maybe it isn't as bad as the media is making it out to be. They always hype things up for ratings."

Picking at some loose trim on the glove box, I can tell he's thinking. "I think it's worse."

Looking at him, I know he's right. I've been trying to avoid that truth, but he's not. I start to say something to try and make him feel better, but stop myself. Instead, I decide to give in. "I know."

We pull up to the school and sit for a moment, looking at each other in silence. There's nothing more to say. We're in a situation beyond our control and all we can do is hope things get back to normal before it gets worse.

Unbuckling, I slide across the seat and hug him. I don't try and tell him it'll be okay, he wouldn't believe me. Instead, I promise to be right here when school gets out. He hugs me back and bravely jumps down from the truck.

Watching him walk away, my chest gets heavy and I realize how much I love my brother. I'll do whatever it takes to protect him. Shaking my head to clear it, I pull away from the curb.

EIGHT

I slide into my first period English seat just as the final bell rings. At the head of the class, our principal, Mr. Sailor, isn't looking good at all. He's written on the board that our regular teacher is out sick.

"Okay everyone, quiet down!" Glaring sternly at those of us in the room, he coughs into the crook of his arm. "I'll be teaching class today. I know things are a bit ... chaotic, but let's try and stick with the schedule as best we can. There are several substitutes here so I expect you to be on your best ..." Coughing again, this time more violently, he halfway stumbles over to the desk in the corner and sits down.

A chiming over the PA system signals the morning announcements. We sit through the regular chatter, say the pledge of allegiance, and then fill Mr. Sailor in on where we left off Friday.

While reading the next chapter in the currently

assigned, typical classic novel, I take the opportunity to look around the room. Close to half of the normally full seats are empty, and of the kids that are here, it looks like a lot of them are in various stages of this flu. I wish once more that I had a mask.

The rest of my morning, classes are much the same. Two out of the four teachers are gone, and one of the remaining ones is obviously sick. There are lots of questions as to why we're even bothering with school, but no one has the answers.

At lunchtime, I get my food and then try to sneak out to the courtyard and as far away from everyone else as possible. Nearly to my goal, I spot Chris walking up quickly to me.

"Alex!" he calls out, even though we've already made eye contact. "Why don't you come sit with me?" Unsure for a moment, I decide there's really no point to evasion anymore. This virus surrounds me. I'm probably literally covered in it. If I'm going to get it, there isn't anything I can do about it now. I follow him back to a nearby table and take a seat.

There are only two other kids eating with us, neither of them friends of mine. Chris tells me their names, but I quickly forget them. I just want to talk with him about my Dad's book, having come to the conclusion that he may be the only person here I can confide in.

Eating slowly, I try to pay attention to the small talk around the table, smiling and nodding at what I think may be the right times. I don't really hear any of it though. The constant noise that's always in this room fills my head, and the smell I have come to lovingly think of as the "cafeteria funk" assaults me. I can't take it anymore. I have to get outside.

Chris has stopped talking and is staring at me. I must not look well, because he seems concerned. Dropping what remains of my sandwich, I stand up and nearly fall backwards over the seat. "I have to go outside," I tell him, walking blindly towards where I think the exit is.

I'm aware of his hand on my elbow, and I'm grateful for his help in finding the door. I haven't had an attack of claustrophobia in years, but I suffered through it long enough to recognize the symptoms.

Trying to slow down my breathing, I sit on the bench outside in the sunshine that Chris leads me to. Once out in the open, I immediately begin to feel better and embarrassment takes its place. "I'm sorry," I say to him sheepishly. "I haven't had that happen in a long time."

"Sorry for what?" Looking at him, it's clear that he's serious. When I don't answer, he moves his hand from my elbow to my shoulder. "Are you okay now? Your color is much better."

"I'm fine. I just needed to get out of there." I look at the trees, the sidewalk, and the other kids ... anything but him.

"Alex," he insists, not giving up.

Finally, I meet his gaze and then find that I can't look away. I'm surprised by what I see there. "I used to get claustrophobic," I explain. "But I thought I was over it. Really, I'm okay now. Thank you."

Satisfied, he leans back, crossing his arms. "How is

your mom today? Any better?"

Forcing myself to break eye contact, I stare down at my hands in my lap. "I guess she's doing better."

"You guess?"

"Well, it's hard to explain. Her flu symptoms are starting to go away, but she doesn't seem like herself. I …"

"What?" He seems genuinely concerned, so I tell him what's on my mind.

"After Dad died, she suffered from depression for a while and had to take some medicine for it. She's been off that for over a year. The way she was back then, sorta like not caring about anything? That's how she seems now, but not exactly." Frustrated at my lack of ability to explain my feelings, I jump right into what I really want to discuss. "What do you think about dreams?"

Blinking at me, trying to keep up with my train of thought, he raises his eyebrows questioningly. "Dreams? What about them?"

"Do you think that, I mean, that it's possible to get a *message* in your dream?" I'm not sure if he understands me, because he sits there staring at me for what seems like forever.

"There are many, many Native American stories and beliefs that surround dreams. You've seen dream catchers?" I nod in response. "That's one example. But it's part of our culture to interpret and listen to what our dreams tell us. As a Christian, I believe that God may use our dreams as one way to speak to us."

This surprises me. That wasn't what I expected to

hear. "Really?"

"Oh yeah, it's very scriptural. I did some research on that due to my cultural background and found that among several other ways God may choose, dreams are a very common one. I think it's somewhere in Job. Umm, maybe thirty-three, that says, 'In a dream, in a vision of the night, when deep sleep falls on people as they slumber in their beds.' I've always liked that verse."

"Wow. That's pretty cool," I admit. "I never knew that kind of stuff was in the Bible."

Laughing, he smiles broadly. "Oh yeah, there's all kinds of stuff like that. You just have to read it. I've done a lot of that lately, in preparation for my mission trip I'm going on after graduation. But why the dream questions?"

Kicking at a piece of dirt that has suddenly become very interesting, I struggle with how to explain it. "What about someone other than God? Like, maybe an angel or a person that died?"

"God uses angels in all sorts of ways and giving messages is one of them. As to an actual person that's died, I don't know. I think there has always been debate about that among Christians. I certainly believe it's possible though. Who's better to serve as your guardian angel than a loved one? Like your dad."

I look at him, grinning at my own transparency. Okay, I need to just jump into this. I look at the clock on the outside wall, only fifteen minutes until class. I'll have to hurry.

"I need to tell you a little about my dad first, if any of

this has a chance of making sense." He nods at me patiently. "Okay, so he was the first in his family to *not* be raised in Egypt. He comes from a very long bloodline of respectable Egyptians. I think it traces back to some king, actually, thousands of years ago. They visited there a lot when Dad was younger so he saw and learned about Egypt; but he never lived there. He majored in history and was a professor for a while, and he was always studying ancient Egypt." Looking sideways at Chris, I see I have his full attention and I'm encouraged to continue.

"Mom and Dad went to Egypt two summers ago for their anniversary. It was a surprise trip that Dad planned out of the blue. You already know he was killed there. Well, Saturday I found this old book left out in his office, and Mom told me yesterday that as he was dying, he told her to give it to me *after* the meteor shower."

"Well that's really weird," Chris says, looking at me very curiously now.

"I know. He had talked a lot about the Holocene shower before, because astronomy was another thing he loved. But I have no idea why it would be so important. Mom said the book was in his bag during the trip, which means he had it there with them in Egypt. It doesn't make any sense. I can't wrap my brain around it."

"What was in the book?"

Turning away from him, I find the dirt clod again. "I wasn't sure at first. It's in Latin. Last night I did some searching on-line and figured out it was titled 'Ancient Egypt History,' which didn't surprise me. There were some hieroglyphics in the text and stuff. Other than that, there were just a bunch of notes my dad wrote all over it, but nothing that means anything to me. Then, last night I had a dream."

Bravely, I meet his eyes now, hoping that he won't think I'm crazy. I tell him about it, all of it. Even the whispers in the woods I heard on Saturday, because for some reason I think it's all related. I finish by explaining how I found the penciled words in the book and what it spelled out. Taking the folded sheet of paper from my pocket, I hand it to him and then sit back to wait for a response.

Chris stares intently at the piece of paper in his hand, brows furrowed. He even turns it over to make sure there isn't anything on the other side. Finally, after what seems like forever, he raises his eyes and meets my own. "I guess we need to figure out where this vulture wants you to go."

A flood of relief washes over me and without thinking, I reach out and hug him. Not one of those nice little A-frame hugs either, but a full out bear hug that almost knocks him off the bench.

Laughing, he steadies himself and I quickly pull away. "I'm sorry!" I gasp, embarrassed. "I've felt so alone these past couple of days and I haven't known what to do. Thank you for helping me."

"That's what friends do, Alex. I think we need to stick together right now. I've been feeling that there is something more going on than appears. I can't quite put my finger on it, but it's there. That your dad seemed to *know* something unusual would happen after the meteor shower, and is apparently now trying to communicate with you about it ... well, we need to learn what it is."

Warmed by his offer of friendship and encouraged to have someone to talk to, I feel much better. Looking quickly at the clock, I see that there's only a couple of more minutes left of lunch. The cafeteria is emptying out as kids march past us on their way to fifth period. "What now?"

"Tonight, you need to rack your brain and try to figure out what he means by that vulture. It seems like the word *hollow* is an important clue. Make out a list of possibilities, anything at all."

"Do you think they'll call off school?" I ask, disappointed to have to wait until tomorrow.

"Definitely. I work in the office second period and they were printing out the letters then. I can't believe they even had us here today. School will be out the rest of the week. I would come over tonight, but I have to go to the church. I've been hearing that several people have died, and we have a lot of older members we need to go check on."

Feeling guilty for being selfish, I sit up a little straighter, making up my mind to take control. "Okay, then. I'll work on that tonight, maybe go through some things in his office, and do some more searching on the internet. Want to meet at my house at about nine tomorrow morning?"

"Sounds good." As he stands to go, the bell rings and the rest of the kids still in the courtyard quickly scurry out, leaving us alone. I tear off the bottom half of the paper with my notes on it and write out my address. Chris takes it, and as we turn to leave in opposite directions, he stops me with a hand on my arm. "Alex," he says.

The tone in his voice makes my heart flutter and I look at him questioningly. "Yes?"

"Be careful." Of what, he doesn't say. Although neither of us can put into words what it is we're fearful of, we both know it's there.

NINE

It turns out Chris was right about the letter. They handed them out the last ten minutes of the day. School is in fact cancelled for the rest of the week.

When I picked Jacob up in the exact spot I promised I'd be, he had a similar note in his hand. He was very excited about it, and all the way home, I heard about how several of his friends either weren't there, or were getting sick. There were still a few unaffected like he was, but it sounded very similar to what was going on at the high school.

Driving past Brent's house, Jacob explains that his younger brother was healthy and at school. He said that Brent was sick but getting better, as well as their dad.

As we pull up to our house, Baxter is at the fence that encloses the backyard, barking happily at us. I go to let him out and pull out my cell phone. I've already checked it several times today, but there's still no answer from Missy. I've only sent her one more message because I figure that if she's able to, she'll get back to me. I'm getting really worried though and decide that if she hasn't texted by six, then I'll call her. Unsettled, I put it back in my pocket and get busy loving on Baxter.

My face covered in dog drool, I follow Jacob into the kitchen. He's at the fridge and getting a snack before I even set my stuff down. Taking the last banana off the counter, I sit down at the table, exhausted. Looking at it, I notice it's a lot browner than its cousin that I ate this morning. Shrugging, I go ahead and peel it. Nothing wrong with a little bruising.

"Ewww, that's gross!" Jacob informs me. He's working on consuming a cold hot dog and I bite my tongue about all the unspeakable ingredients *he's* eating.

"I guess we need to go to the store soon." Tossing the banana skin in the garbage, I eat the last bite and go to the freezer. "One more pizza in here. We can have that tonight and I'll go shopping tomorrow."

Jake is more than happy with the evening's menu and he and Baxter disappear out the back door. I watch them leave and smile at his ability to adapt. Then I realize that Jacob didn't even ask about Mom, or go check on her. Is that part of the coping mechanism? He's normally what you would call a momma's boy. I find myself frowning again.

Taking my own cue, I head down the hallway. Why am I so apprehensive? Am I afraid that she's going to be worse? No, I admit. I'm fearful that she'll be the *same*.

I find her door closed, and so knock lightly before

opening it. She's propped up in bed with the television on. One of the many crossword puzzle books is in her lap and she's tapping a pen on her forehead, deep in thought. Maybe that was why she didn't call out a greeting when she heard us come inside?

Standing in the open doorway, I wait for her to acknowledge me. There are dirty dishes on the nightstand and empty bottles of water on the floor, so she obviously felt well enough to get up and find food. That's good, right?

"Mom?" I say, when the silence draws out until it's awkward.

"Hmmmmm?" Still absorbed in the puzzle, she doesn't even look at me.

"We're home from school. Lots of people are sick though, so they cancelled it for the rest of the week." When she doesn't answer, I try again. "You look like you're feeling better. Can I get you anything?"

Finally, Mom lowers the pen and faces me. Her eyes look sunken, the skin around her nose raw. Her expression is so neutral that I can't tell how she feels. "I'm getting better. I just ate though so no, I don't need anything. Call your Grandma Fisher back though. I didn't feel like talking to her."

I see now that one of the home phones is on the bed next to her. Didn't feel like talking to her? Slowly, I walk forward and pick it up. I also grab the dirty dishes and empty water bottles. I try and catch her eye again, to look for any sign of normalcy, but her nose is turned back to the puzzle.

I make my way from the room and towards the kitchen, my arms full. "Alex, close the door." I stop mid-stride at her voice. Closing my eyes, I take a deep breath, then go to the sink, and dump everything in it.

Going back to her room, I quickly close the door before I have to look at her again, shutting it a bit more loudly than I meant to. When she doesn't comment on the slamming, I run to the end of the hall and into my own bedroom. As an afterthought, I slam *my* door too, against this stupid flu, against Mom's weird behavior and the note in my pocket that both excites and scares me at the same time.

Throwing myself on the bed, trying to deal with my upwelling emotions, I realize that I still have the home phone in my right hand. I stare at it for several minutes and finally push the buttons to call my grandma. I'm not sure what I'll say to her, but maybe they can come out and stay with us for a little while if I explain what's going on.

When Grandma answers the phone on the fourth ring, my heart drops. Her voice is barely recognizable and I know without a doubt that she is sick. Really sick. "Grandma!" I practically yell, tears springing to my eyes.

"Oh, Alex honey, how are you? Are you and Jacob still okay?" The effort to talk makes her cough and I wipe at the tears that have spilled over onto my cheeks.

"We're fine, Grandma, really. You sound sick though."

"Yes, both Grandpa and I have been hit pretty hard. We got the antiviral meds today though. I went in to the doctors this morning and he got us started at the first sign of this flu. Dr. Carl is good at that kind of stuff, you know. But your Aunt Tammy is very stubborn. She insists that staying at home and washing her hands is going to keep her healthy."

I talk with her for a while, until she is coughing so much that she has to go. I don't even mention Mom's odd behavior or needing her to come out. There's no doubt that it's not possible now. Telling her I love both her and Grandpa, we say goodbye.

After hanging up I decide that my idea to wait until six to text Missy is stupid. I pull out my cell phone and call, praying that she'll answer. It goes to voicemail before the first ring is finished, indicating that her phone is off. Frustrated, I go to my desk and dig out my small address/phone book. Looking up her home phone, I dial that one and close my eyes.

I open them in surprise when her dad answers it. Relief flooding me, I ask to please speak with Missy. There is an odd, muffled sound and I assume he is covering the mouthpiece. I can hear muted, indistinct conversation and then my relief turns to dread as he tells me that Missy doesn't want to talk right now.

"Doesn't want to talk?" I repeat back to him, confused. "Is she that sick?"

"No. She's getting better. We'll all be okay now."

When he doesn't offer any further explanation, I'm at a loss as to what to say. "Well, can you please tell her I'd like to talk with her as soon as ... she wants to?"

"She knows. Goodbye." The line goes dead and I'm

left staring at my cell phone like it's a snake about to bite me. I throw it away from me, trying to distance myself from this new, bizarre reality.

Tears blurring my vision, I stumble off the bed and to the computer. Not knowing what else to do, I log on to my social account to see if there is any sort of talk from others about people acting weird. I can message Missy too, in case it's her dad and not her saying that. Waiting for the site to come up, I impatiently tap on my desk. When a message pops on the screen stating that the page is temporarily unavailable, my sadness turns to anger.

In one sweeping gesture, I knock all the papers, notebooks, and pens off the surface of the desk and onto the floor. Not satisfied, I grab at pillows and blankets and throw them across the room. Turning in a circle, I look for something else to destroy and catch my image in the mirror over the dresser.

My thick black hair is in disarray, my face streaked with tears. What stops me though is the cold, hard panic in my eyes. They're black with fear and unrecognizable to me.

"Alexandria, the vulture ..."

Staggering backwards, I spin around, looking for the source of the whispered words. Clasping both hands over my ears, I fall to my knees on the pile of pillows. "What do you want me to do?" I cry out, my voice a hoarse imitation of itself.

I have no idea how long I'm in this position, weeping quietly. When I finally open my eyes, I'm wrapped up in the same fluffy comforter Mom had given me at the meteor shower. This brings on a fresh course of emotions and I am about to close my eyes again when I notice a book that is practically under my face. Pushing up onto my elbows, I look at it.

Sure enough, it's Dad's book. I have no idea how it could have gotten here. Thinking back, I'm almost positive I put it back in its hiding place this morning and I don't think my temper tantrum took me into the closet. Looking at it more closely, I see that it's open to the page where my dad carefully drew out the vulture in pencil. The vulture.

Accepting the fact that this is the new normal, I sit cross-legged and try to figure out what it is Dad's trying to tell me. I'm not alone. He's with me, I know it with all my heart. Chris is there too, and willing to help. What is absolutely clear is that I'm not doing anyone any good lying here crying on my bedroom floor.

Wiping my face on the blanket, I push down all those raw emotions. I'm sixteen, practically an adult. My little brother is counting on me to take care of him and it seems that Dad had enough faith in me to trust me with whatever this is all about.

I reach out and pick up one of the pads of paper and pens that are now littering my bedroom floor. Across the top, I draw out some lines making three columns. At the top of each column, I write: *Holocene meteor shower, weird stuff* and *vulture*.

I start with the meteor shower. Under the heading, I start making notes: every five thousand years, Dad very interested, Dad knew something was going to happen afterwards, mentioned to Mom when dying, happened same night as flu starts, much more intense than scientists said it would be, was strongest in our region, meteors crashed near town.

Then under the weird stuff: Flu, Mom not acting like herself, more than being sick? Missy won't talk to me, spreading like wildfire through country, highest contagion rate in history? Dad's book, dream, whispers, Baxter acting strange, something is "off."

Finally, I come to the vulture: the drawing in the book, in my dream, whispered to me, I have seen it somewhere else before. In this house?

I pause, pen poised over the paper. I have? Yes, I have. I *know* I have and not in a book, either, but *on* something. Something of Dad's, something ... I jump to my feet.

"Something I've touched!" I say out loud, running for my door, tripping over pillows as I go.

Going to Dad's office, I can hear a loud video game being played in the family room. Content that Jacob is accounted for, I open the door and go inside, closing it behind me. Turning on the main light, I stand staring at the rifles on the wall in the same spot they were the other day.

Crossing the room quietly, I carefully lift the top one down. The one Dad taught me how to shoot with, the one with the elaborate carvings on the wooden stock. Pointing the muzzle down, I hold the stock up to the light to inspect the lines. Among other stick animals and patterns there is the hieroglyph of a vulture.

My heart beating faster, I tip the rifle upside down and look at the end of the butt. Yes, there is an endplate held in place by two tiny screws.

Going to the desk, I rummage through the drawers until I come up with a small Phillips screwdriver. Slowly, I unscrew them, making sure not to strip them. Once both are removed, I tug on the cap and it comes off easily in my hand.

Nicely folded and tucked away in the small hollowed-out stock, is an old piece of paper. Hardly believing my luck, I pull it out and immediately put it in my back pocket. My heart slamming to the point that I'm sure it'll be heard in the next room, I replace the endplate as fast as I can. Not sure why I feel such an urgency to cover my tracks, I place the rifle back on the wall and turn out the light, leaving the office in a hurry.

Once in the hallway my heart rate begins to slow, and as I get control of my breathing, I realize I'm nearly hyperventilating. Sweaty and a little dizzy, I go to the kitchen for some water, noting that Mom's bedroom door is still closed.

With glass in hand, I walk through to the family room to check on Jake. Acutely aware of the paper in my pocket, I still feel a need to make sure he's okay.

I find him sprawled out on the couch, this time chasing mushrooms and jumping on stars, with Baxter snuggled up to his side. He raises his big brown doggie eyes as I walk up, and then whimpers at me. It's an odd sound, a mixture of his begging for food and "I want outside" plea. It's as if *he* isn't sure how he should feel, either. Relating to his inner conflict, I lovingly rub his ears and tell him again that he's a good dog. This settles him a bit and he lays his head back on Jacob's legs.

"I'm hungry, Alex, when are you gonna make the pizza?"

Well his appetite is normal, so that's a good thing. Looking at the clock, I'm surprised to see that it's already close to five. "I'll put it in now. We can eat in half an hour. Does that sound good to you?"

"Sure," he answers, groaning when he apparently loses his last life. "How's Mom?" Setting the controller aside, he seems troubled about asking the question. Like he already knows the answer, but doesn't want to hear it.

"She's getting over the flu, but I don't know if she's up to having dinner with us. I'll ask her." Smiling, I try to seem upbeat. I told him the truth ... just not everything. He must be satisfied with the answer because he goes back to his game.

After pre-heating the oven, I place the pizza in to cook and find some frozen garlic bread to stick in with it. I definitely have to go grocery shopping tomorrow. Grabbing a bottle of water from the fridge, I decide to try to talk with Mom again, see if she wants to eat with us.

I turn on the hall light as I go, pushing back against the darkness that is already starting to fill the house. At her bedroom door, I knock again before opening it.

The curtains are drawn to block the fading sunshine outside, and the TV is off. My shadow stretches across the floor, projected by the light behind me. I can barely make out her shape in the bed. "Mom?" I whisper, not wanting to wake her if she is really asleep.

Slowly, she turns towards me, and I gasp as her eyes meet mine. In the gloom, I could swear that they're reflecting the light back at me! It's almost as if they're *shining* like the eyes of a cat. Taking an unsteady step backwards, I rub at my own eyes, convinced that I must be mistaken. Blinking sleepily at me, I'm held captive by her gaze until she lies back in the bed and her glowing eyes disappear.

TEN

Three hours later, I'm finally alone in my room. Jacob is tucked away in bed watching a movie with Baxter on duty as guard. I'm amazed that I made it through dinner and a couple of hours of mindless re-runs.

It seems that all the normal programming has been changed to last year's episodes without explanation. The news hour was limited to what's new in Hollywood as of last month, the weather, and very little new info on the flu. Only that it's "wide-spread." I noticed the newsman looked quite sick.

Finally unable to take it anymore, I had ushered Jacob to bed early and escaped. I kept touching my pocket to make sure the faint outline of paper was still there, like it would disappear.

Now that I have the privacy I need to examine the note, I'm a little scared. I have this feeling that I've fallen down the rabbit hole and that once I take this next step, there's no turning back.

I've almost convinced myself that what I saw earlier was my imagination. Almost. I'm sure there must be some logical explanation, like a play of light or something. My mind can't grasp any other possibilities and recognizing that I'm at my limit, I decide to put off thinking about Mom until tomorrow, in the daylight.

I take my time in re-making the bed, arranging the pillows on it and folding the extra blankets. Turning my attention to the mess on the floor, I put everything back in its place on the desk. I need some order if I'm going to keep my sanity.

Making myself comfortable in the pile of pillows, my back against the wall, I take a deep breath and take the paper out of my pocket. I start to unfold it but stop, unable to get over my unease about the unlocked door. I'm convinced it's going to open at any moment. Jacob might have Baxter, but I'm all alone.

Making up my mind, I jump up and go to the desk. Grabbing the straight-backed wooden chair, I drag it across the floor. It's an old one I found at a yard sale a few years ago. Mom thought it was horrendous, but I love the antique, heavy wooden frame. I added a nice big overstuffed seat cushion and it was perfect for my room. Now, as I wedge it under my doorknob, I'm extra thankful I had made the purchase.

Feeling better, I go back to the bed and settle in again. Pulling at the corners of the browning, thick paper, the first thing I see is what looks like an old wooden coin nestled in the middle. Picking it up, I hold it under the lamp on my nightstand so I can see it better. It *is* wooden, but definitely not a regular coin. It looks to be incredibly old. It's almost a quarter inch thick, flat, smooth on one side, and expertly carved on the other. The carving is raised, like it could be used to make an imprint or something. I carefully study the picture and although old, it is still distinguishable. A pyramid is in the background, all three corners touching the edge and slightly raised. Inside the pyramid, looking out at me is an intricate skull, the eyes filled with radiating lines like sunshine. Numerous lines also go out from the pyramid in all directions seeming to represent light. There is a small hole in the top of the pyramid and I imagine it's meant to be worn as a necklace. Perplexed, I set it gingerly aside, finish opening the paper, and set it in front of me, pressing out the creases. I recognize the handwriting immediately as my father's and begin reading:

Alexis, I'm writing this for you in case something happens and I'm unable to carry this out myself. If you are, in fact, reading this then it means you were able to decipher my first message. I apologize for the secrecy but it is necessary. It also means that I am gone and for that I am so sorry, but know that I will never really leave you.

I'm afraid that I still can't give you any real information. If I did and it was read by anyone other than you, the consequences could be catastrophic for the world.

*Alexis, you **must** understand that you **cannot** trust anyone who is or has been sick. <u>No one</u>. The flu outbreak will be the result of a virus carried here by the Holocene meteor shower. It was*

carefully designed and its intent is evil.
Don't give up Alex, I love you-
Dad

Yup. Down, down the rabbit hole I go. No stopping now. Closing my eyes against the rising panic, I will the room to stop spinning and take deep slow breaths. I picture the fishing hole, sunshine reflecting off the surface, birds chirping happily. Back to a time when things were right and I felt safe.

The imagery works and once I feel in control I open my eyes. The note and medallion are still there. It's real. Reading it again, it's less shocking and so I read it a third time, and then a fourth.

The implication of what it says weighs heavily on me. He knew he might die, which tells me that his death probably *wasn't* random. He obviously felt that whatever it was he knew would have an effect on the whole world. Well, I put that thought aside to come back to. I don't have any possibilities for what it means right now.

The one thing made clear is that the meteor shower and the flu *are* connected. This actually makes me grin as I think back to Saturday when Jacob, in his childish wisdom, had already figured it out. Maybe I was wrong to not involve him from the beginning.

My grin quickly fades as I consider his warning. So my instincts were right. This flu virus is doing more than making people sick; it's *changing* them. Its intent is evil. How? What is it doing?

Running my fingers through my hair, I focus on the

ceiling, searching for answers. He wouldn't be leading me on this path except for one of two reasons: to protect me and help me get away from it, or he knows how to fight it.

His words indicate that other people were searching for the knowledge he had and were willing to kill for it. This tells me that it's more important than protecting me. *Catastrophic for the world.* No, this isn't just about me.

With a newfound resolve I look at the rest of the note, which consists of a string of hieroglyphics:

I'm at a loss. While one of the pictures looks like a man with a bow and another one a bird, I have no idea what the other pictures are or what any of them represent. Dad had explained to me what hieroglyphics were: the alphabet for Ancient Egyptians. It dates back to more than 5,000 years ago. There are ones used for straight translations, some that are phonic and others that are grouped together to mean different things. But I certainly don't know how to read it.

Of course, Dad would have known that. I'm thinking he chose ones that will be easy to figure out. However, anyone with the right book or a computer could do the same thing, so I'm guessing that whatever it "says" is meant to mean something only to me.

Sighing, I become resolved to the fact that I am bound to be frustrated. But I get up anyways and go to the computer, not wanting to wait until tomorrow to look these up. I pull over a big beanbag from a corner to replace the chair.

First, I try to again to log on to my social account with the hope that I can contact Missy. The same message flashes up and I'm not surprised. I check my email and see that the inbox is empty. Curious, I hop back onto the conspiracy message board. Normally incredibly active, I'm alarmed to see that most of the threads are almost a day old and it's been hours in between some of the responses. For some reason this change really hits home for me how widespread this is.

I don't have the patience right now to read through any of it, but I take note that it might end up as a great resource for getting un-filtered information from other people around the world.

A quick search takes me to a site packed full of Egyptian hieroglyphics and their meanings. But what had seemed like an easy enough task is apparently much more involved than I thought. The vulture is the only common one. It's the equivalent to the A in our alphabet and can also refer to "mother," "queen," or in ancient Sumerian times "father." Hmmmm … I know which one *I'm* going with.

The other pictures are not so obvious. It takes me about two hours and several other websites, but I finally have what I think to be a pretty accurate translation scribbled out:

I spend another half an hour searching through various combinations of images that include pyramids and skulls. When I don't come up with anything useful, I throw in the word wooden coin, then medallion and carving. While there are a whole lot of interesting things, there's nothing even close to the medallion I'm holding. My eyes burning, I turn off the computer and get my pajamas on as the words tumble around in my head. *Chosen, to go out; leave, mountains, forest, archer, duck in flight, burial.*

I dig around in my jewelry box until I come up with an old necklace on a long chain. I remove the worthless pendant and string it through the medallion. I slip it over my head, and feeling the weight of it against my chest, somehow makes me feel closer to my dad.

I check in on Jake, who is asleep with the TV on. Turning it off, I make sure the small light in his closet is on and the door ajar. It isn't technically a night light, but he gets panicked if he wakes up in the dark.

Baxter watches me as I move around the room and licks my hand when I pull the covers up around Jacob's chest. I reach out to pet his head, but then decide I need a doggy hug instead. I spend a few minutes there cheek to cheek, silently soaking up his calming, unlimited love.

By the time I get back to my room and wedge the chair back under the handle, I am beyond tired. Falling into bed, I hug one of my pillows to me and press my face into it. A headache is threatening in my forehead and I know the stress is catching up with me.

Just as I had suspected, the message doesn't mean anything to me ... yet. I'm determined to figure it out and I know Dad chose those images for a reason.

I'm looking forward to seeing Chris in the morning

and showing him everything I discovered. I had thought about texting him but Dad's warning has gotten me very paranoid. Better to be on the cautious side I think and not do or say anything over the phone or internet. This is best explained in person anyways.

The creaking of a door out in the hall reaches me and I sit up in bed, suddenly wide awake. Tiptoeing to the door, I press an ear against it. It would be very unusual for Jake to get up.

I hear soft footsteps on the carpeted floor heading towards the kitchen. There is the unmistakable sound of dishes and glassware banging around and then more footsteps coming back.

Silence. Bent over at the waist, my back screaming now in protest, I am frozen with my head up against the door. I have a vivid image of Mom standing out there, paused in the doorway to her own room. I know without a doubt that she is there, and that she is also aware of my presence.

After what seems like an eternity, the door creaks again and then closes. Muffled sounds of the television seep out into the night and I relax enough to go back to bed.

Grasping the same pillow as before, but very tightly, I pull a blanket up over my head like I used to as a little girl. Leaving an opening just large enough to let in fresh air, I lay in the darkness and wait for morning to come.

ELEVEN

Sometime during the night, I must have fallen asleep, because the next thing I know the much-awaited sunshine is bathing my pillow. The blanket is off my face, probably pulled down at some point when I was unable to breathe. The raw fear of the night before has faded, but it remains as a dull ache in the pit of my stomach.

Looking at the clock, I see that I even slept in, since I didn't have to turn the alarm on the night before. It's almost eight. Deciding I may as well get up, I put my sweats on and remove the chair from in front of the door.

Unplugging my phone, I check to make sure I haven't missed any texts. I briefly consider trying Missy again, but I don't feel like I can deal with the cold rejection right now so I put it off. I'll give her another day and try again tonight or tomorrow morning.

I find Jacob and Baxter sound asleep, wrapped up

together so that it's hard to tell where one ends and the other begins. Just the way it ought to be.

It dawns on me that I haven't had a shower in over two days, and I head for the bathroom. After a brief time I re-emerge fresh and clean. As I stand there, trying to muster up the courage to go into Mom's room, I hear noise from the kitchen. Startled, I check Jake's room again and confirm he's still there.

Walking cautiously to the kitchen, I stop at the entrance and watch Mom in silence. I have a rush of hope as I see her washed up and dressed in her normal work clothes. In fact, she looks absolutely radiant.

She's at the stove cooking something. Based on the smell, I'm guessing bacon and eggs. Bread pops up out of the toaster and as she turns to get them, she sees me. If she was surprised, it doesn't register on her face.

"Alex. Good morning. Breakfast will be ready in a few minutes."

She smiles at me then and all my hope turns to dread. It's a false smile, one that curls her lips but doesn't get anywhere near her eyes. In fact, her eyes are a much darker blue than usual and I notice that it's because they are dilated slightly more than they should be. However, they aren't glowing and for that, I am very thankful.

It's the way a teacher smiles at you before handing you a test back with an F on it. It's not my mom's smile. She's a loving, caring person that is always concerned about us. I don't know who this person staring at me is, and that smile scares me more than anything else up to now.

"Thank you," I say evenly, feeling like I have to be careful in how I answer. "You're going to work?"

"Yes." Moving with an ease and grace I've never seen in her before, she transfers the food to two plates and sets them on the table. "Get your brother up. I'll be back later."

My feet feel frozen to the floor and I just look at the food. You need to understand that Mom hardly *ever* cooks. When she does, the results are nowhere near what I'm seeing. The last couple of times that she made eggs, I pretended to eat and then gave them to Baxter. I honestly don't know how she messes them up so badly. Bacon is always cooked in the microwave to avoid the fire alarm going off. Last time I had pan-fried bacon was when Grandma Fisher was over.

The food set out on the table looks like it's been prepared for a magazine photo shoot. I look back at her and cringe when I see the same cold expression on her face.

"Okay. I need to go shopping." I don't know what else to say.

Turning briskly away from me she sweeps her purse up. "You still have my bank card, use it." Stopping in the open doorway as if an important thought just crossed her mind, she tilts her head to the side. "How have you been Alex? You don't seem sick," she asks, without turning around.

Instinct takes over and I answer without any hesitation. "I started to get a horrible sore throat last night and this morning I'm all achy. I think I'll spend most of today in bed."

She stays poised in that odd stance for another moment and then leaves without another word. I stare at the closed door until I hear the garage open and I see her Honda pull out onto the street through the kitchen window.

I realize I'm holding my breath, and let it out with a gasp. Dad's warning echo's in my head: *You cannot trust anyone who is or has been sick. No one.*

Sitting at the table, I absently pick up a fork and start eating the eggs. Is the Mom I know and love gone forever? Pushing that thought back I look down and find that most of the eggs on the plate are gone. If anything else had made me suspicious, the fact that those were the best scrambled eggs I've eaten in my life confirms it. My appetite gone, I grab both of the plates and dump the food. I won't let Jacob see this.

In need of answers, I go to her room. She's been closed up in here for three days now. I don't know what time she got up at this morning, but I suspect that she's been awake since I heard her last night. The room is spotless, the bed made and all her laundry done. She's not a sloppy person, but I have never seen her room this put together before.

Carefully stacked on her nightstand are the four crossword puzzle books I got for her. Removing the top one, I randomly flip through the pages. No. It's not possible. I look at the whole thing and then pick up the next one. My fear growing, I grab the third and then the fourth. They're all the same. Every single one of them.

Sliding down the side of her bed, I sit on the floor, the books scattered about me. One is open and I stare accusingly at the filled in spaces of the puzzle. *All* the spaces. Mom has never finished a puzzle before. Ever. She doesn't even look up the answers because she thinks it's cheating. I have always thought it was funny when she would try to do one, but she insists that it helps with brain function. She sees so much dementia and Alzheimer's among her patients, that she'll do anything she can to not get it herself.

So how is it possible that *every single* puzzle is completed? Not only that, but her handwriting is perfect. It almost looks like it's typed. So much so that I had to wipe at the ink to make sure it smeared. Her penmanship isn't usually as bad as a doctor's, but it's not what you'd call nice.

This isn't my mom. The thought seeps in and then resounds in my mind, like it's not my own. That I am almost able to accept it scares me. Pushing at the books, I shove them away from me, not wanting to see what's in them.

After several minutes, I numbly gather them up and carefully place them back exactly the way they were. I'm more determined than ever to figure out what's going on and how I can stop it. Until then, I think that being paranoid is a good survival instinct.

TWELVE

Chris shows up a short time later, just after nine. The knock at the front door makes me jump even though I'm expecting it.

The last of the frozen waffles made an adequate breakfast for Jacob and he's eating them hungrily in the family room while watching TV. He's approaching the whole thing like a mini vacation and is actually in a good mood. He hasn't even asked anything about Mom, after I told him that she had gone to work and was doing better. I wish I could ignore everything too, but that isn't possible.

Answering the door, I wonder how I look when he smiles at me and wish it had occurred to me *before* he got here. For the second time now, I don't have any make-up on and my hair is simply brushed out and loose. He probably thinks I only have these one pair of sweats and old t-shirt. Although I am a bit tall for a girl, he is still several inches taller than me and I look up at him shyly. I toy with the idea of running to my room and changing, but figure that would be way too obvious.

Inviting him inside, I remember the reason why he's here and all of a sudden, my vanity seems pretty silly. I'm sure he couldn't care less anyways.

Jacob gives us a suspicious look as we walk by, but he doesn't say anything. I'll tell him a convincing story later, like we're working on something for school. I hadn't given it any thought and I'm not good at making stuff up real quick. I make note of this lack of planning and sense that I need to get better at it real soon.

Leading Chris into my dad's office, I take a seat at the desk, leaving the chair against the far wall for him to sit in. I have the old book and list of words out on the desk, which he's already seen. Next to it is the paper I removed from the rifle.

"So last night I figured it out," I say, jumping right to the point.

Chris seems surprised and leans forward eagerly in his chair. "So? What was it?"

Picking up the paper, I hand it to him and then point up at the rifle. "I took your advice and made out some lists. It stirred up some memories for me and I realized that I had seen that vulture somewhere else. After thinking about it, I finally remembered the carvings on the butt of my dad's old rifle. That one."

He follows my finger and looks at the weapon. Standing, he walks over to it and inspects the wood. "Do you mind?" he asks, gesturing to pick it up.

"No, go ahead. It's not loaded."

Removing it from its hooks, he handles it like someone who is familiar with guns. Keeping the muzzle pointed down at all times, he inspects the decorative etchings and then looks at the butt plate. "Hollow!" he says, understanding immediately how it all ties together.

"Yes," I confirm, "and that paper was inside. I already deciphered it. The writing off to the side is mine."

Replacing the rifle, he sits back down and spends some time reading the message. After several minutes, he finally looks up. "He must have written this just before he was killed. That was what, over two years ago?"

His expression is neutral, but he's gone a bit pale. The dark fear that's been threatening to engulf me intensifies and I try to push it back down.

"Yes," I answer evenly. "He died two years ago last month. So it was sometime before that."

"He somehow knew that this virus outbreak was going to happen, and that it would be at the same time as the Holocene meteor shower. How is that possible?"

I stare at him, unable to give an answer. I'm somewhat relieved to see that he's just as confused by this as I am.

"… In case I'm unable to carry this out myself." Chris reads from the paper to make sure he's quoting it right. "Carry *what* out? This implies that it's all about *you* finishing some sort of mission for him. That it has to do with the virus, and that the virus was pre-planned, or at least known about. It might not even be from earth if it was on the meteors." I remain silent, letting him work through it all on his own.

"Its intent is evil. Intent? So how in the world did your dad know about a designed virus with some sort of evil purpose arriving in a meteor shower that only comes around every 5,000 years? What does *any* of this have to do with you? I'm guessing these secrets might have gotten him killed, and he knew that it might, which is why he had this backup plan. I don't know, Alex." Shaking his head, he stands up and begins pacing. "This is just too much. I mean, I'll admit that this virus has been incredibly contagious and vicious and that there's some odd behavior going on ever since ... but this?" he says, holding out the paper. "This is a whole lot weirder than any of that."

"Oh, I agree with you," I say, still in my seat watching him pace. "I would like to ignore it all and pretend like everything is okay, like my little brother out in the other room. However, as you just pointed out, Dad somehow *knew* this was going to happen. What that tells me is that no matter how bizarre and unlikely this may all seem, he was *right*. He was right, Chris. And ... my mom *has* changed."

Stopping in the middle of the room, he looks at me carefully. "What do you mean? Depressed, like you were telling me yesterday?"

"No. She isn't depressed." I tell him about her behavior last night and this morning, trying to stress how peculiar it all was. When I describe the crosswords, I know it might seem like I'm making a big issue out of something small, but I'm hoping he gets the larger picture. I hesitate about her eyes, but finally give in and tell him, taking a chance he'll just decide that I'm crazy and leave.

When I finish talking, I study his face to gauge his reaction. He's good at guarding his emotions; I really can't tell *what* he's thinking. "You're right," he says with resolve, as if he's made up his mind. He sits back down across from me.

"I am?" I was expecting more of a debate.

"We can't ignore the *fact* that he knew this was going to happen, or that people who get sick are changing. If we accept that reality, than we also have to admit that something huge is happening that your dad was somehow involved in. Big enough that he was killed for it and is now trying to guide you from the grave."

I want to hug him again, but this time I stop myself. I'm relieved that he believes me but also scared that we're right. I need to figure out what to do next. "So now what? I don't know what those hieroglyphs are supposed to mean."

Chris looks back at the images and my translation. "It must mean something to you," he says, handing it back to me, "or else your dad wouldn't have written it."

"I know! That's what I keep telling myself, but I don't get it. I mean, am I supposed to leave here and go find a soldier and tell him everything to keep from dying? But then, what's the duck and who's the soldier? The army, FBI or even the police force he worked for? Maybe someone on the department knows. I've been thinking about everyone he used to work with and if the duck reference could mean one of them, but I'm not coming up with anything." Tucking my hair behind my ears, I finally stand up, taking over the pacing for him.

"I don't think it would be that broad of a reference, Alex," he says, watching me. "I think he carefully wrote something that would only make sense to *you*. A personal reference. Think smaller."

Completely discouraged, I sit back down and hold my head in my hands. "I can't think straight anymore," I say, my voice muffled.

Kneeling down in front of me, getting to eye level, he takes a hold of my wrists and I feel obligated to look at him. "I don't blame you. It's a lot to deal with. I think you need a break from this for a while. Maybe it'll help clear your thoughts."

"I need to go shopping," is all I can say in return.

Laughing, he pulls me to my feet. "Okay, then let's go shopping. I'll help."

"Oh, wait!" I say, remembering the medallion around my neck. Pulling the chain over my head, I place it in his hand. "This was inside the paper. I have no idea what it is."

He rolls it around in his hand for a minute and then looks closely at the image. "I've seen some things similar to this for secret societies, like the Illuminati. Pyramids are popular for that kind of stuff, but I don't remember seeing anything quite like this. It looks really old. Maybe it was even used for making seals. You know, like in wax on sealed envelopes? That would explain why it's so raised. It's interesting, that's for sure. Might tie into what kind of organization your dad was involved in."

The thought that Dad was part of some secret group doesn't make me feel any better. I put the necklace back on and tuck it out of site. "Maybe it'll make sense at some point. Right now, I don't have a clue. Let's go."

Jake stays home for brief periods of time quite often, but I'm still hesitant to leave him behind. When I invite him, he insists that he'll be fine and doesn't want to go. Sure that Mom will be gone for several more hours, I give in and let him stay.

Chris wants to take his car, a small white sedan. On the way to the store, I go ahead and ask if he's heard anything from his mom.

"No. It's been almost a month now." He continues to stare straight ahead and at first, I think that's all he's going to say. "Not many people know this, but six months ago, she got a new boyfriend who was into drugs. Heroin, actually."

Not knowing what to say to that, I watch the trees pass by out my window, sorry now that I asked.

"She met him at the real estate office she worked in. He seemed like a nice enough guy at first, but I caught on real quick. I tried to warn her, and then to get her to break it off with him, but by then it was too late. I found her shooting up one morning and when I got home that afternoon from school, she was gone. Not even a note. I don't think she plans on coming back for a while, because she packed quite a few things. Took most of the electronics too, I figure to pawn to buy more drugs."

Turning to look at him now, I wonder how he's

managed to keep everything together. I guess in a way, we've both lost our parents. Reaching out, I rest my hand on top on his. "I'm sorry, Chris."

It sounds so inadequate, but I know there isn't anything that I can say that will make that kind of hurt any better.

Shrugging, he briefly grasps my hand and then puts it back on the wheel. "What can I do? I just hope she's all right, wherever she is, and that she'll find some sort of redemption."

We ride in silence the rest of the way to the store, our moods somber. Today, the parking lot isn't nearly as full as it was on Sunday. I spot Mr. Jones's old red Chevy pickup out front and my hopes rise a little.

As soon as we enter the store, I can see him at the front, elevated counter using the register. There are several people waiting to be helped though, so I decide to talk with him when we're done shopping.

Wishing now that I had taken the time to write out a list, we make our way up and down the aisles, tossing things in that look good as we go by. I know that I'm forgetting stuff, but probably won't figure out what until I get back home.

After more than half an hour and a nearly full cart, we find a place in line and wait our turn. There are only a couple of people ahead of us so it isn't long before I'm standing in front of Mr. Jones.

Happy to see him, I give him a big smile, but before I can talk, he curtly asks me if there'll be anything else I need. My feelings a little hurt; I tell him I need four pounds of ground beef.

Watching him work, I find that coldness seeping out from my center that I have come to associate with fear. Well into his seventies, he's normally a bit slow at the tedious task of tying up a pack of meat, his arthritic hands a bother. His speech has become less clear the past few years too and Mom had told me that dementia was starting to set in, which explained his talking more slowly and being a little absent minded.

Today however, his hands move quickly and smoothly like those of a teenager. When he barks out some orders to another store employee at the same time, he is clear and more coherent than I've ever seen him.

"How is Mrs. Jones?" I ask, not seeing her anywhere and hoping that perhaps she is still herself.

"She died Sunday night." He says it with such a complete lack of emotion that I actually take a step backwards and collide with Chris. Here is a man that absolutely adored his wife, literally cherished the ground she walked on and he is telling me about her death like it was a squirrel that got ran over. I stare at him with my mouth open, eyes wide.

His hands stop as he obviously registers my surprise, but doesn't acknowledge it. Slowly, he starts wrapping the butcher paper again. "So, Alex. How have *you* been feeling?" he asks, head tilted slightly to the side and without looking at me.

Desperately fighting the urge to run from the store, I realize I may have made a big mistake. Chris's hands are on my arms, where they stayed after stopping me from my backward shuffle. They tighten ever so slightly, indicating his awareness of the danger too.

"Actually, Jacob and I are both sick now." I try to say it convincingly and absently grab a package of cough drops from the front counter rack, adding them to the pile of groceries.

Ignoring my answer, he silently finishes the meat order and rings everything up. Chris bags it all for me, just as eager as I am to get out of here.

As Mr. Jones hands me back the check card, he holds on for a moment longer than he should, tugging a little. Looking up at him, our eyes meet. Like Mom's, his are slightly dilated and I feel like a rat caught in a trap.

Assaulting me with that same, lifeless smile, he lets go of the card. "Hopefully you'll be feeling okay soon," he says, watching me carefully.

As we calmly walk out of the store, several customers turn to stare at us simultaneously. Afraid to look back, we almost run out the exit, knowing without a doubt that we're still being watched.

THIRTEEN

I wake up late Tuesday night to Baxter barking. Falling out of bed, I stub my toe on the chair that I forgot was wedged under the doorknob. By the time I have it opened I'm wide awake, hopping in pain, and convinced someone is in the hallway waiting to kill me.

Instead, I find Mom standing near her bedroom door, eyes slightly luminescent in the dim light. I'm not sure whether to feel relieved or not.

I'm caught in her stare like a deer in the headlights and Baxter comes over to cower by my feet. Ignoring us, she simply walks into her room and closes the door without saying a word. No explanation of why she's home from work so late, no hello ... nothing.

Stroking his head with much more confidence than I feel, I calm Baxter down to the point where he's okay to leave the hallway and go back to Jake's room. However, I don't sleep much the rest of the night.

At ten the next morning, Chris sends me a text saying he needs to talk with me ASAP. Mom left a note on the table in the kitchen saying that she would be going back to work at two today, so I tell Chris to come over at 2:30.

Mom hasn't gotten up yet, and neither has Jake. Going quietly into his room, I close the door and sit on the edge of his bed. He's watching SpongeBob and I get caught up in the story before I can stop myself. When the commercials come on, he mutes it and looks at me expectantly.

"Jake, I need to talk with you about something, but it's going to sound a little strange," I say to him softly in a guarded tone. He seems perplexed, but I have his attention and so I continue. "You know that almost everyone has been getting sick and that you and I are part of a small number left that didn't get the flu." He nods his head slowly, not sure where I'm going with this. "I can't explain why, but I need you to pretend like you're sick now, too. Both of us need to, even with Mom."

I look at him, waiting for a reaction. To my surprise, he agrees with me. "I know," he says evenly. "Something is wrong with them. They aren't the same anymore. I think we were all supposed to change, but we didn't and so now we're ... like, wrong. So yeah, we need to make them think we're like them."

I study his face, trying to figure out how he got so smart. "What made you think that?" I finally ask him.

"Well, because of Mom. And, don't get mad, but when you were gone yesterday shopping I went over to

Brent's." I bite my tongue, holding back a lecture so he'll continue with his story. "He was different, too. So were his parents. They looked at me funny, like they didn't know me or didn't like me or something. Brent didn't even want to talk with me or hang out or anything, Alex. It was like it wasn't even him. They asked me twice if I was sick, if I was okay. I lied."

His eyes are welling up now and he looks down at Baxter, concentrating on rubbing his ears. I reach out and grasp his chin, lifting his face. "I'm glad that you lied, Jake. It was okay this time. I'm not mad you went over. I would have too, if I were you. Missy is acting the same way, and her parents. It isn't just here, it's everywhere."

Throwing his arms around my neck, he buries his face in my hair. Hugging him back fiercely, we stay like this for some time.

"I want to go to Grandma and Grandpa Fishers," he finally whispers, pulling away. His eyes are dry and I can tell he's trying to be brave, but I don't want to burden him with too much at once and wonder if I should tell him the truth.

"I talked with Grandma Monday night and they were both sick," I say, deciding that being honest was the best way to handle things right now. "I'll call them again tonight, though. Maybe it isn't as bad that far away or maybe Aunt Tammy is all right. It sounded like she might have still been okay."

"I want Mom back." He doesn't look at me when he says it, and takes a big shuddering breath.

"I know Jake, I do too. I'm going to try and find a

way to make her better." I can tell he's dejected and want to offer him something reassuring. "Look, if Grandma and Grandpa are better or if Aunt Tammy is okay I'll ask if we can go visit, okay? I'll find a way to get there, but either way we're all going to be all right."

"Promise?" he asks, looking up at me again. His eyes. Those dark, loving, trusting eyes. I can't let him down. I nod my head, a new sense of determination and resolve filling me.

"What you need to do today though, is just stay in bed. At least until Mom leaves for work. She came home late last night and is still sleeping, but she'll be leaving by two. If she checks in on you, act like you have a really bad cold and fever. Can you do that?"

"Yeah, I can do that. Can I watch TV?"

"Of course you can," I say, amazed again at his resiliency. I ruffle his hair and he actually gives me a small smile. I smile back, feeling better.

Leaving his room, my chest aches with the love I feel for my little brother. I know that as long as we stick together, we can figure this out. Mom can't help how she's acting; she's sick. The normal flu symptoms might be gone, but there is obviously something more involved happening. I just have to find a way to make her better. I'm beginning to believe that the best way to do that is to follow the trail Dad left me.

Back in my room, I see that it's already eleven. Taking my own advice, I put on my big fluffy robe. Grabbing some Kleenex, I stick a few in the front pocket and go out to the kitchen to find the cough drops I bought. Just the smell of those makes me think of a sick person.

By the time Mom emerges around one, I'm situated on the family room couch with soda and crackers, propped up watching old re-runs of "Little House on the Prairie." If this doesn't convince her, I don't know what will.

"Not feeling well, Alex?" she asks, right next to my head. I'm not sure how long she's been standing there, but it scares the heck out of me. Jumping what I swear is about a foot, I look back at her. Her hair is yet again styled to perfection, the blonde curls pinned back from her face. Her work scrubs are pressed and much neater than I've ever seen them.

Doing my best to look tired and achy, I blow my nose as loud as I can without being too fake. "Yeah, I'm feeling pretty crummy today. Worse than yesterday. So is Jacob."

She just stares at me. I try hard not to squirm. As the silence drags out I become convinced that she's trying to decide what side dish to eat with me, and I have to say something. "So, I called Grandma back like you asked. She's sick and so is Grandpa. Missy is too, but she won't talk to me anymore." I look at her, hoping to see some glimmer of emotion cross her face. Nothing.

"Your grandparents should be fine. They have no serious underlying medical issues. Same for Missy. As they get to feeling … better, I imagine they will have more important things to do than have idle conversations that mean nothing." As those words sink in, she cocks her head to the side in that odd, questioning gesture again. I'm beginning to regret my attempt at a conversation, but figure I may as well keep digging.

"It sounds like pretty much everyone is getting sick. You seem to be fine now, except that Jacob and I miss talking to you, Mom." I bravely stare back at her, challenging her, and then remember to wipe at my nose.

The briefest glimpse of a smile, no, more like a *smirk* creeps into her mouth and her white teeth glisten wet between her thin lips. Regret for my boldness tugs at me and I begin to pray for that neutral expression to come back.

"It appears to have an eighty percent contagion rate, perhaps higher after all the secondary infections turn up. The death rate is about ten percent at our hospital, but only with those having other issues like diabetes, heart conditions, and such. It's a very efficient virus."

Her last comment chills me and I feel relief when she turns around and walks into the kitchen. "I won't be home until late again," she explains. "There is … a lot of important work to be done at the hospital."

The sound of pots, pans, and cupboards opening and closing goes on for so long that I carefully peek over the back of the couch. Blinking fiercely, my mind tries to grasp what I'm seeing. She is moving with such speed and agility that at first it doesn't make sense, like I'm watching a cooking show in fast motion. During the time she was banging around, there is already a large bowl of what looks to be a chef salad, some sandwiches stacked up, and something cooking on the stove. It smells delicious. Now she is doing the dishes. The rate at which she is literally throwing the plates into the washer is startling and I mean actually *tossing* them down after rinsing them. They are landing perfectly in between the tongs that hold them in place, one after the other.

Slowly, I lower my head and lay back down on the couch. I don't want to see anymore. I don't want to hear anymore. I want her to leave. Taking slow, regular breaths, I look at the TV and desperately try to get lost in the world of wagons, farming and simpler times.

Finally, after what seems like an eternity but was really only ten minutes, Mom comes back to the family room holding her purse and a small lunch cooler. "I'm leaving now. I left you enough food for tonight and tomorrow." When I don't answer, she turns to go but then comes back and sits on the small coffee table right in front of me.

Wanting to pull the blanket over my head, I instead meet her gaze. "Alex," she says, reaching out and picking up the bag of cough drops that's lying next to me. "You be sure to get well now." Slowly, she reaches in and pulls one out, rolling it in between her fingers like a magician with a quarter, all the while studying my face. "I wouldn't want you to become part of the ten percent."

Standing abruptly, she drops the bag and the single cough drop on my chest, then takes her stuff, and leaves without another word. Looking at the medicine like it's poison, I pull the blanket over my face, wanting to block it all out, but not finding comfort in it anymore.

FOURTEEN

When Chris knocks on the door an hour later, I'm still under the blanket. I don't know if I dozed off or not, but Baxter's barking brings me up for air.

This time when I let him in, I don't give any thought to how I look in my big robe and ponytail. It's the least of my concerns. Based on his expression when I first see him, it's obvious he has bigger things on his mind, too.

We walk silently into the family room and I turn the television off. Picking up all the loose Kleenex and cough drops, I make room for us to sit on the couch. "Pretending to be sick?" he asks, looking at the array of things next to the couch.

"Well that was the plan, but Mom pretty much called my bluff and then implied that I might die because of it. I'm thinking I don't need to pretend anymore." He stares at me in astonishment, so I tell him exactly what happened.

"I guess today is the day for crazy encounters with our moms," he tells me, shaking his head.

"What, your mom came home?" I'm hoping for something positive but fearing the worst. "What happened?"

"So you know that she hasn't been here for a month. Last time I saw her she was high on heroin and a total mess. She had lost her job, her hair was starting to fall out, and her skin was all marked up." Standing, he walks over to the sliding glass door and looks out into the backyard as he continues talking. "This morning, I'm sitting in the kitchen eating the last of the Cheerios when she comes walking in. She looked great, I mean better than I've ever seen her. So there I am with the spoon halfway to my mouth, surprised and confused because she just walks right past me like she'd gone out to get milk." He turns around, and I see the obvious anguish on his handsome face.

"Alex, I know how you're feeling now. She started getting ready for a job that I didn't know she still had, saying only a few words and not expressing any kind of remorse or love towards me. I tried to talk to her and she stared at me like I was a fly or something. It seemed to dawn on her at some point that I was confused by her behavior. All she said was that she's obviously back, like I was an idiot, and then asked me if I'd been sick. I told her I was getting over it and went to my room until she left. It's so bizarre that I don't even know how I should feel."

Sitting back down beside me, we face each other.

"We have to do something, Alex, but I don't know what. Everyone I was close to has changed, even the pastor."

Feeling for him, I take his hand. "We haven't changed Chris. I believe there's a reason why we haven't. We'll figure it out and find a way to help them."

Smiling slightly, he stands back up. "I know you're right. I think I just needed to hear it. That reminds me," Taking some folded papers from his back pocket, he hands them to me and then sits in the easy chair across from me.

"What's this?" I ask, unfolding them and looking at the printed sheets.

"I decided to do some research last night on viruses. See what it is we might be up against. I went over to the library and used the computers there, since mine is gone. What I found is pretty amazing and scary at the same time."

Science isn't really one of my strengths and I don't have the patience right now to wade through the technical details. "So give it to me in plain English," I request.

"Well, basically the science world can't agree on whether viruses are a life form or not. Really doesn't matter, I guess. Anyways, it's basically this very tiny ball of either bits of RNA or DNA with a protective coating around it. It can get into your body several ways, but the most common is airborne, then blood borne."

"Some of that I already knew, but not the being a life form part. That's creepy," I tell him, nibbling on the crackers left out and going stale already.

"Well, the best part is how they work. They attach

themselves to your cells and then drill inside, release the bits of data and literally hi-jack the little building machines inside it. It makes your cells build replicas of its own information until the cell is full and then bursts open, releasing all the new viruses to spread out and repeat the process."

"Ewww. Where does the DNA or RNA come from that it puts in our cells?" I ask, intrigued now.

"No one knows," he answers. "That's where our current virus comes in. I'm thinking it's not too far of a stretch to suggest that there really *could* have been viruses on those meteors. In fact, it has been theorized before. What's encouraging is that with enough time, vaccines can be created for some of them, but obviously not all, like HIV."

"The problem with that," I interject, "Is my mom just told me that at least eighty percent of the population is being infected, maybe more. I don't think that anyone who's changed is going to be interested in creating a cure. They seem very content. How do you think it's changing their personality?"

"I've been wondering about that," Chris says. "If these things have bits of DNA in them, and are known for crossing the blood-brain barrier, how crazy is it to assume that they can affect different parts of the brain, say the thinking section or feelings? I believe we're seeing a new form of super-virus that is more complex and with greater effects than any other ever experienced."

The phone rings and we both jump, staring at the receiver as if it was someone that snuck into the room.

Leaning over to the end of the couch, I snatch it off the receiver. "Hello?" I ask, but realize right away it's an automated message from the school district. To my surprise, it's a recording saying that school will be in normal session starting tomorrow, Thursday.

Chris is staring at me questioningly as I hang up. "It was the school. We have to go back tomorrow." I don't know why that bothers me so much. Maybe it's because the new norm is becoming the reality and those of us unaffected are now the outsiders. I don't like the feeling. "What do we do?" I ask him.

"Go to school. At least for the rest of this week. Lay low, learn as much as we can and of course, figure out your dad's message. Any luck with it?"

Exhaling, I try to hide my frustration. "Well, not thinking about it for the rest of the day yesterday didn't work. So, I stared at it for a couple of hours before going to bed. Nothing new came to me. I was hoping I might have another dream last night, but I slept horrible the first half and hardly at all the second. No dreams that I remember. I'm not sure what to do about it."

"Where is it?"

Going to my closet, I get the folded up paper from the book, from under the bear. Opening it, I hope to have a revelation but I disappoint myself again. Plopping heavily back down on the couch, I lay it on the table between us.

For the next two hours, we make lists of all the different things the hieroglyphs might be referring to. I go on-line at one point and look up the roster for the police department, hoping to be inspired, but there isn't anything obvious that connects any of them to the clues. We try reversing it, mixing them around, and any other number of varieties. As time drags on and my patience wears thin, the weight of what could be at stake bears down on me.

"Let's give it a rest for today." I think Chris can tell it's taking a toll on me.

"Sure," I say, happy to agree. "Want some lunch?"

"I would, but there are still some families left on my list that I need to check. The pastor and other senior members that I know were all sick. Out of my youth group, only one other leader was uninfected. There were four of us. Two of the fifteen kids are okay, but both have one parent sick. Or maybe by now they aren't sick anymore either, I haven't seen them since Monday."

"Do you need help?" I ask, not sure what I could do, but feeling like I should offer.

"Thanks, Alex, but that's okay. I'm meeting with Kevin, one of the other leaders, in a little bit at the library and we're going to figure out who else we need to check on. I think there are only three or four families left so it won't take—" Before he can finish, the phone interrupts him.

Figuring it's the school again (we often get two calls since Jake and I go to different schools) I answer it without saying anything. "Is this Alex?" A man asks when I don't say hello. His voice is very deep with a slight, guttural accent similar to my Grandpa Mubarak's. I look at the caller ID and see that it's a blocked number.

"Yes, this is Alex," I answer quickly, somehow knowing that this is important.

"Listen to me *very* carefully, Alex. You must go where you are being led. It is imperative that you listen to anything your father is telling you regarding the current …. situation. Do you understand?" he asks with urgency.

I recognize the voice, but I'm not sure from where. It is so distinct that I feel like I should know, but for the life of me, I can't remember. "I understand," I tell him, feeling a need to keep it vague. "I'm listening." There is a deep sigh on the other end of the line. Relief? Then it goes dead and I'm left staring at the receiver, more confused than ever.

Chris is watching me with interest and I tell him what was said. "This just keeps getting stranger," he says. "I guess we at least know that we're not completely alone. Maybe this guy will be able to help us, if he decides to."

We agree to meet in the cafeteria in the morning before class, and then say goodbye. Going back to the couch, I'm not sure what to do with myself. I feel like I'm wasting precious time.

Reaching for my cell phone, I go ahead and call Missy. It goes straight to voicemail again. I pull up Grandma's number and give her a call next. It rings four times and I'm about to hang up when the line is picked up.

"Hello?" I ask when I don't hear anyone on the other end.

"Yes." It sounds like her.

"Grandma?" I question, any hopes I had dashed.

"This is Mrs. Fisher. What is it that you want, Alex?"

"I was checking to see if you and Grandpa were feeling better." I try to hold back the tears, but I don't seem to have any control over them.

"We're okay now. Everyone is okay." The line goes dead and I am left staring in disbelief. They're gone to me now, too. I put the phone down and exchange it for some of the tissue.

I get myself together and go make dinner, just going through the motions. I keep it simple. The salad and sandwiches Mom made are in the garbage.

After feeding Jacob, who is still happy to be holed up in his room, I retreat to my own. I decide to do a little digging myself on the internet. There's no way that Chris and I are the only ones to have figured out that something is very, very wrong. If I weren't so spooked, I would just call our family doctor, but Dad's warning was very clear.

The official news sites are all the same. Literally. Exactly the same stories word for word. My unease grows. The social sites are still down and my email is empty. What strikes me the most is the lack of spam.

The only mention of the flu now is that it reached the East Coast but is quickly dying out. Those without complications have almost a full recovery in around four days. The death rate is, in fact, ten percent. Great.

I figure the message boards are my best bet so I log onto the conspiracy site again. It doesn't take me long to figure out there's less than half the normal traffic. I'm suspicious that a lot of it is fluff, or stories just posted under different users names, but not really them. I've been a member for over a year and have become familiar with several of them. It doesn't feel right.

After spending some time reading through a bunch of threads, I'm sure that I'm right. They're making it appear normal for anyone left that cares. There are a ton of members that are from other countries. I'm guessing the virus hasn't spread *that* far yet, and I would expect to see all sorts of conspiracy theories popping up from them. Perhaps they're being erased as fast as they're posted.

As if to prove me right, the next time I refresh the page, I see an interesting title at the top of the forum: *Shiners; side effect of virus or real change?* I click onto it as fast as I can, before it disappears.

The author is a long-time member whose writing I have always enjoyed. He's one of those guys who obviously takes his time and researches stuff before giving an opinion, and doesn't jump to conclusions or get too worked up about things. It's almost like finding out an old friend is still there and I feel relieved to know he's still himself.

As I eagerly read it, for the first time today I feel encouraged. He's writing from somewhere in Europe and apparently, the flu has just started creeping up in spots but is spreading rapidly. They've had the time though to observe what was happening in the States before the media blackout and internet control. Groups have started to form in advance of the virus and are trying to avoid infection by bunkering down. They have begun calling those infected "Shiners," due to their eyes glowing in the dark. It's suspected that among several other attributes, they have enhanced night vision, much like cats, which causes their eyes to reflect the light.

No one claims to know what the infection really is, but they made the connection to the meteor shower and that it's alien. It increases all five senses as well as overall IQ, while at the same time making them uncaring and nearly emotionless.

The only other observation that was news to me was that the attribute unique to those *not* infected was their race. Or rather, percentage and purity of race. It all made sense now. Jake and I are both fifty percent Egyptian and Chris is like seventy-five percent Okanagan Indian. I guess if the virus targets DNA, then it would all tie into that somehow. We have greater resistance to the infection and maybe even immunity because of our heritage.

I type out a response as soon as I finish reading. I tell him that about eighty percent or more are infected and that the assessments of the symptoms are accurate. I suggest that if they can't isolate themselves, they should take off for an unpopulated area.

I hit enter and then immediately regret it. I should have printed the post out first. My worst fears are confirmed, as I look at the list of threads after the page is done refreshing. Not there. I try to go back to it, but get a 404 message. Doing a search, I find another old thread authored by him and try to send him a private message. Selecting his profile, it comes up as banned. Well, that's it then.

Dejected, I sit back in my chair. Shiners. Having it all confirmed makes the reality of it set in even more. It's spreading around the world. People are changing everywhere. Somehow, my father knew this would happen and it has now fallen on me to do something about it.

A whining behind me gets my attention and I turn around to see Baxter sitting patiently at my door. "Whatchya need boy?" I ask. In response, he runs back down the hall and disappears around the corner.

Groaning a little, I pull myself up and follow. In the family room, I find him sitting at the coffee table. Figuring he's helping himself to the rest of the crackers, I get ready to scold him. To my surprise, when I crouch down next to him I find the page with hieroglyphs under his nose, the food ignored.

I look at him, and he returns my gaze. Most dogs will look away immediately, but not Baxter. He's always been like that, but tonight he seems even more determined to win this contest. "Okay, okay," I say, kissing him on the nose. "I won't give up."

FIFTEEN

I'm back in a dream world. I'm sitting cross-legged on a chilly dirt floor in a large cave. The room is dim, lit only by some torches scattered around the rock walls. Although I can't see the top, I am aware of its immense height and can hear the beating of wings far above me in the blackness.

The smell of damp earth mingles with wood smoke and I notice a small stream running between the far wall and me. Looking up, I catch a glimmer of movement and turn to my right in time to see the same vulture from before swooping down. Silently gliding in one large circle, it heads for the wall, and before I can call out, slams into it. But instead of hearing a thud, the vulture explodes out as if made of mist, which is then absorbed into the rock.

Once the mist is gone, I see that left on the wall behind it is the same hieroglyphic drawing from the note, the one that means mountains. Leaning towards it, I squint, trying to see it clearly. I'm convinced that the lines of the picture are starting to move. The motion becomes more exaggerated and it's obvious that the dark lines *are* in fact unraveling and slithering across the rock. More curious than alarmed, I watch in fascination as they dance around each other and eventually form the archer hieroglyph.

I gasp as the archer leaps away from the wall, landing in the dirt not twenty feet from me, swinging his bow and arrow back and forth, looking for prey. As it begins to walk along the creek, the bow morphs into a rifle and he shifts it to his shoulder. Turning quickly in my direction, he aims the rifle above my head and I look to see what he is hunting. Coming in low over the water is the duck from the message, quacking as it passes over me.

A shot rings out and I jump at the sound. Looking back at the archer, I see that he's splashing through the water towards his fallen prey. Before he reaches the duck, another loud sound explodes, causing me to jump again. It is a grating sound, like a horn, and it blasts over and over, echoing through the cave.

I fight to keep the vision, but it fades into grayness to be replaced by my room in early morning light. Opening my eyes all the way, I'm disoriented for a moment, until I realize that my alarm is going off. Slamming my hand down on it almost hard enough to knock it off the nightstand, I can't believe my bad luck. I almost had it!

Sitting on the edge of the bed, I tap at my forehead,

trying to remember everything I saw. A vulture flying into the picture of mountains, an archer shooting an arrow ... no, a gun at the duck. Pushing away from the bed, I run to my closet and get the paper. At my desk, I turn it over and write out my dream on the back of it. I don't want to forget any details.

Looking back at the culprit clock, I can't believe what time it is. It must have gone off a couple of times. I'm irritated that I have to go to school, but I know it's the best chance of buying us some more time and possibly figuring some other things out, like who else isn't sick.

Jacob got pretty upset last night when I told him about school. He was terrified of facing everyone there that's changed. After Mom called last night and said she was pulling a double shift and sleeping at the hospital, I gave in and told him he didn't have to go. She won't be back until tonight and we'll tell the school he's still sick. We can probably get away with that for at least today and tomorrow. That'll give us the weekend to plan what to do next.

I rush to get ready and make Jacob breakfast, waking him up when I set it next to his bed. I let Baxter out for his morning outing and then drive reluctantly to school.

I manage to make it into the cafeteria by the designated time and to my relief I see Chris right away. Without saying a word, he turns and starts to walk towards the same exit we went through on Monday for the courtyard. As we wind our way through the tables, I notice for the first time how unusually quiet it is. The room is almost as full as on a normal day, but the constant din I find so annoying is gone.

A bit flustered, I look around at everyone. Aside from a small group clustered together at a table in a far corner, the rest are either reading, writing or eating quietly. To my dismay, I realize they are all watching us as we walk through. I quickly avert my gaze and try to wear a neutral expression, but I can feel the weight of their eyes on my back.

Once outside, Chris crosses over to the bench furthest away and I follow without a word. There are only a few other students in the yard, but they are on the opposite side talking loudly. One of them, a girl from my science class named Heather, is openly crying, and waving her arms around. One of the other kids is trying to calm her down, shushing her, and looking around them, obviously scared.

"What do we do?" I whisper to Chris, afraid to even look at him. Instead, I sit down stiffly and remove one of my books from my backpack. Setting it in my lap, I pretend to be studying it.

"Just make it through the day. Act like them, no matter what. We don't want to draw attention to ourselves. Avoid any emotional displays, even a smile. We have no idea what's going to happen next. It could get worse, or it may be nothing. I mean, maybe this will eventually wear off, and they'll all go back to normal."

I cling to those words, hoping that they're true. In my heart though, and that part of me that I guess you would call instinct, tells me otherwise. ... *You cannot trust anyone who is or has been sick ... It was carefully designed and its intent is evil.* My dad's words of caution come to mind and I know that we are in danger, no matter how much we want everything to be okay.

"No," I tell him. "Its intent is evil, Chris. That's what my dad said and I believe him. We both know this is all in preparation for something else." I take a chance and look at him, to find him already watching me.

"Right," he finally says, looking back down at his hands. "I've been thinking and praying about that a lot and what it might mean."

"Well?" I ask, not sure if I want to hear what he has to say.

"I wish I had an answer for you, but I don't. Other than I agree with your dad. This is born from something evil, not of God. What you said yesterday though stuck with me. There's a reason that we have been left unaffected. I think we have a role to play in all of this and when our faith is tested, we have to believe that love will prevail."

"I'm not sure what faith is, to be honest with you Chris. But I'll take all the help we can get, so if you think God is listening, then say a prayer for me too, next time."

"I already did," he tells me, taking a textbook out also. More kids are walking by now, as it gets closer to class time.

"Maybe that's why I had another dream this morning," I say and hand him the paper with the details written out on the back. He studies it silently and then gives it back. I quickly put it away.

"Mean anything to you?" he asks, a hopeful note in

his voice.

Not wanting to disappoint him, I try to stay positive. "I really haven't had time to think about it. There's something that's tugging at me the same way the picture of the vulture did. Something familiar, like a distant memory that's a bit faded. I just can't quite put my finger on it."

He's nodding his head as if I've said something meaningful. "That's good! Like I said, I think it is something personal that will only make sense to you. We better get going," he continues, putting away his books. "I have a feeling that the only people rushing in before the bell rings will be those of us that haven't been sick."

Suddenly scared, I stand up timidly and sling my backpack over my shoulder. "I feel so alone here, Chris. What if they figure it out?"

"I did some math," he says, keeping his back to the walkway. "There are around 500 students, so if eighty percent got sick, that means there should be about a hundred of us here that are still normal. There should be a couple of other students in each class in the same position we are, so you aren't alone. Just don't talk to them. I know you'll want to and I'm going to try and keep a list of everyone I'm familiar with so we can contact them later. But not here at school."

"Okay," I whisper, practicing my emotionless expression. "Meet me at my house after school? My mom won't be home until late." Nodding, he walks away and I head in the direction of my first class.

The morning is a mixture of weirdness and fear. I

swear my heart is going over a hundred beats a minute the whole time and I am fighting to hold it all in. When I walk into first period, everyone already seated turns simultaneously to look at me. I continue to head for my assigned seat and manage not to meet any of their gazes.

After I sit down, they all face the head of the class where Ms. Easton is standing. I do my best to mimic them and sit staring at her. Just when I think my chest is about to burst, the bell finally rings. Going to her desk, she directs everyone to come forward to get their new reading assignment.

Trying to hide my normally very expressive face, I take my place in the orderly line that's forming and get the book. Sitting back down, I read the title; "A Guide to Socialism: How to Implement it and be Successful." Okay, not your typical assignment.

There's a disturbance in the back of the class and I do my best to turn my head in time with the others. Chris was right. Tim and Matt, two guys that are always running late, have pushed through the door. They're standing there, disheveled and obviously upset.

Under the watchful eyes of the whole class, they walk slowly through the room and sit down, a bit dazed. "Tim. Matt. Come and get your new reading assignments," Ms. Easton says evenly.

They obey without a word and to my relief no one lifts their heads to observe them. "What the hell?" Matt says, disgusted. I cringe at his voice but then quickly recover, trying to see him without moving my head. He's holding the book out to the teacher, obviously upset about the change of subject matter.

"Matt, you will remove yourself immediately to the nurse's office," she tells him, snatching the book out of his hand. "You're obviously not feeling well." She was on her feet and standing in front of him before I even realized it.

Matt was taken by surprise by her speed too, because he stumbles back several feet and then leaves without another word. Tim goes to his seat and starts reading, having decided it was best to blend in.

The next three classes are much the same but without any outbursts. It was easy for me to pick out the other students that were like me, because they didn't know yet what was at stake. Most of them were complying, but noticeably concerned. I saw several kids trying to leave the school in between class, but they were being stopped at the doors by staff and led to the front office.

I have been trying to find and talk with some of my friends throughout the day who are normal. In art class, there are three girls from my soccer team. Two of them I know well and as soon as I determine that Lisa isn't a Shiner, I start planning on how I can slip her a note. I manage to get a message scribbled down and am waiting for us to be told to get our clay projects out. As I'm working up the nerve to do it, she walks over to one of the other girls that is a close friend of hers and makes the disastrous decision to plead with her. I watch in despair as Lisa starts crying and the teacher quickly intercedes, ushering her out of the classroom.

I try not to think about where she went and just make it through the rest of the class. Ten minutes before the bell is to ring for lunch, my art teacher hands out a simple questionnaire. There are only three questions; have you been infected with the super flu. Have your family members been infected with the super flu. List the names of any family members that have not been infected yet. My pulse quickening again, I answer yes to the first two and leave the last one blank. I don't want to get sent to the office too.

We're handing them back in and the speakers chime, indicating the first announcement for the day. I have a bad feeling about this.

"All students and staff will report immediately to the auditorium for a mandatory assembly," Principal Sailor states with authority.

Without a word, everyone stands at once as if on cue and I join them, walking single file through the halls towards the gym. At the entrance, we are held up as my teacher hands the stack of answered surveys to someone standing there. After a few minutes, they call out three names. I watch as they fall out of line and hesitantly move forward. They are ushered over to another door and the rest of us continue inside and into the bleachers.

Once seated, I copy those around me and place my hands loosely in my lap, back straight, eyes straight ahead. There are already several hundred of us here, but the large room is eerily quiet. There are a few coughs and a random sneeze but no talking, no shuffling of feet.

Across the gym and on the other end, the kids whose

names are being called out gather. While quieter than usual, they are still much louder than the rest of us. They are sitting in groups and talking amongst themselves, some hugging, others are crying. I long to be with them, one of the normal ones. I need the physical contact and comfort that they are giving each other. But at the same time, I have a very bad feeling that's getting worse by the minute. This can't be good.

A few minutes later, the last class makes its way into the stands and I'm relieved to see Chris with them. They sit several rows below us and as soon as they settle in, Mr. Sailor strides out to the center of the room.

He stands there for a minute, surveying us, and I'm convinced he's going to call out my name and send me to the other side. However, he simply clears his throat and addresses us all. "Thank you for your co-operation. Class is dismissed for the rest of the day. It will resume at its normal time tomorrow." He turns to the normal kids. "You will stay here." Then back to us. "That is all."

As he begins to walk away, four hundred students stand as one and we quietly leave the gym in the same order we entered. Caught up in the tide of motion, I take a chance and turn to look back at the group still seated on the other side.

I can see teachers with their hands up, holding them back and telling them to stay seated. As I reach the exit, I notice Heather mixed in with them and her eyes meet mine. I will never forget her fear and my inability to do anything about it.

SIXTEEN

Chris pretty much follows me home and I'm glad for the company. The whole scene has left me a little shaken. All I can think about is what's going to happen to them. Breaking a rule, I turn my phone on as I'm driving. I try calling one of the police officers that's stayed close to our family, but when he answers, it's clear that he's changed. I don't know who else to turn to. I claim to have dialed a wrong number and quickly hang up.

As I pull into the driveway, it dawns on me that if Jacob hadn't made a fuss about it, he would have been at school today, and I'm pretty sure that something similar happened there. The thought causes me to panic and I literally run from the truck and into the house, needing to make sure he's all right.

"Jacob!" I yell, heading for his room.

"What! What's wrong?" he calls out from the family room. I spin around and go back the other way, having missed him in my rush. He's lounging on the couch and has been playing video games, but he's dropped the controller in alarm at my voice.

"Oh!" is all I can say, kneeling down next to him and giving him a hug. I fight back the tears and manage to smile instead. "Nothing is wrong, I was just afraid you might have left the house again after I went to school. Things are weird and I don't want you out there. You were right to stay home today."

First concern and then hope crosses his face. "Does that mean I don't have to go tomorrow?" he asks.

"Definitely," I tell him. The sound of footsteps causes me to look up and I see that Chris has come inside. "Hey, Jake, do you think you could give us a few minutes?" I ask. "We need to talk about ... school."

"Sure," he says good-naturedly, jumping up off the couch. "You made me fall into a pit anyways." Tossing the controller onto the couch, he calls Baxter to him and goes out the back patio door after saying hi to Chris.

"He's a good kid," Chris comments, watching Jacob and Baxter run around the back yard.

"I know. I can't stop thinking about what might be happening to him right now if I had made him go to school."

"Maybe nothing," Chris counters, sitting down next to me. "We just don't know. They could all be back at school tomorrow." We look at each other silently, neither one of us wanting to put into words any other possibility. It's just too hard to contemplate or acknowledge.

I tell him about my failed phone call, afraid I might

have drawn more attention to us. He also admits to calling his friend's parent.

"I saw Kevin over there in the gym, Alex. I had to do something. His dad answered and when I explained it to him, do you want to know what he said? *'Don't worry Chris, he'll be okay now. How are you feeling?'* I hung up." Silence settles over us, the atmosphere heavy.

I take out the sheet of paper with my dream's description on it, and we start to talk about that instead. For some reason I focus on caves and if there are any in the area, while Chris is convinced the stream and rifle are key elements. After less than an hour, his cell phone rings and to his surprise it's his mother.

"Hello?" he says hesitantly, while shrugging at me. His expression changes from uncertain to bewildered. "I'm at a friend's house. They had a schoolbook that I need." He listens for another minute, his frown deepening. "Oka—" But apparently the call is cut off, because he doesn't get to finish.

"What was that all about?" I ask, as he sits staring at his phone, deep in thought.

"I'm not sure. She asked where I was and wanted to know why I wasn't at home. This is the first time since coming back that Mom has even showed an interest in me. She's acting like there's something planned that I know I'm missing, but there isn't. I don't even know why she's home this early. The office doesn't close until five."

"She hung up on you?" I press, a little worried about his situation. Maybe Kevin's dad called her.

"Kind of. She said to come home now and hung up

before I could even answer. I don't know, Alex. I should probably do what she says if I don't want to raise even more suspicion."

"Yeah, I guess. But leave if there's anything too strange, okay? And will you text me later and let me know you're all right?" I feel silly after saying it, but I'm finding that my friendship with him is part of a very thin thread holding me together right now. It wouldn't take much to break it.

"Oh, don't worry about it. I'm not going to stick around if I feel threatened. As far as texting, I don't think we should do it anymore. I was thinking about that earlier today. If there is some sort of mass organization happening among the people that are infected, they might have the ability to track or monitor us.

"Maybe I'm being a little paranoid, but I haven't seen hardly anyone using their cell phones or any other electronics. Have you? Maybe computers, but none of the hand-held devices. It's almost like they're already synced and don't need to text or communicate that way anymore."

His comments remind me of the thread I read, so I tell him about it while he gets his backpack. "So I don't think you're being paranoid, it's probably a smart idea." I comment as he goes out to his car. "Can you just call me briefly then on the home phone?"

Smiling, he gets in his Honda and starts it up. "I'll call you, don't worry. We'll see each other tomorrow, and we can compare our lists after school. We need to start contacting other normal people over the weekend. We have to figure out what to do and where to go. Let me know if you interpret the dream or message, because I think that'll be the key to it all."

Nodding, I wave as he drives away and go back to the house. As I get to the door, I notice Jacob and Baxter standing nearby. Jake's looking at me strangely and it makes me wonder how much he overheard.

He follows me inside and hovers as I go to the fridge. "What were you guys talking about?" he asks, sitting at the kitchen table. "What dream?"

Getting some water, I turn to face him. He's looking at me expectantly, and I'm conflicted over whether to involve him in it or not. A pressure on my foot gets my attention and I look down to see Baxter sitting on it. He's looking up at me with such wide eyes that it startles me. A low, back-of-the-throat growl builds in him until he barks once at me. He's never behaved this way.

"Okay," I whisper at him. "I get it." Satisfied, he moves away and goes back to Jacob, lying at his feet.

Jake doesn't quite know what to make of it and is looking back and forth between Baxter and me. "Get what?" he asks.

"Jacob, I have a question for you. That dream we were talking about? I had it last night. I believe that someone is trying to tell me something in my dreams. But I'm having a hard time figuring it out."

"Tell you something about what?"

"About what's happening with the flu and Mom and why people are acting so weird," I try to explain.

"Oh. All right. So tell me about it."

His ease at accepting what I told him makes me envious. Why can't it be that simple for me? "So, Jake, you know what hieroglyphics are, right? The ancient picture words that Dad told us about?" When he nods, I continue. "So if Dad were to draw out a series of hieroglyphs meant to tell me something that basically said: Chosen, go out or leave, mountains, forest, archer, duck in flight, burial. What do you think it would mean?"

He looks at me with a blank expression. "It says what?"

Trying not to get discouraged, I get the paper from the family room and place it on the table in front of him. "Here, these are the pictures. I wrote out beside it what it means. Maybe it'll help if I tell you my dream?"

He studies the pictures, his brow knitted in concentration. "I think you should just tell me your dream," he says in agreement.

I explain it in detail, everything I can remember. When I'm done, I can tell that something has caught his interest. "Why did you say that this was from Dad?" he asks.

"I don't understand it all myself Jake, but I found an old book of Dad's that had a message in it for me. That's how I found that note. So I believe that he's trying to tell me something. Chris thinks that it will only make sense to me. That it's a personal reference between Dad and me. You were always a part of our time together too, though. So what do you think? How is an archer with a gun, shooting a duck, relevant to us?"

His face brightens and he jumps up from the table.

"I know!" he says excitedly, grabbing my arms. "It's totally obvious!" he yells, hopping up and down.

My hope's rising, I can't believe it was that easy. "What?" I demand, his energy rubbing off on me. I can't help but jump around with him.

"The duck blind of course!" he says, spreading his hands in a "duh" motion. "He wants you to go to the duck blind!"

Yes! That's it, he's right. Relief sweeps through me and I understand now why there was something familiar about it all. I hug Jacob and pick him up off his feet, spinning him around the kitchen, both of us laughing. Baxter gets excited too and starts prancing around us barking.

"How could I have been so stupid?" I ask no one in particular. "And why didn't I ask you sooner?" I say to Jacob, his smile making his pride apparent.

Several years ago, after Jake was born, my dad built this incredibly good duck blind. He took Jake and me hunting there many times over the years, but neither of us has gone back since his death. Mom hates hunting, so she's never seen it. I don't think she even knows what it is, let alone where.

One of the now retired lieutenants on the police force owns the fifty acres of hunting land a couple of miles from our house. To get to it, you drive to a trailhead and then hike or bike another mile to a less worn trail. This takes you back to a stream and wetland area. From there it's another un-marked trek into the woods and the duck blind. It's built from surrounding material but very solid. We spent many hours huddled in there, waiting and watching for the ducks. There must be something buried there, hence the burial hieroglyph.

Filled with hope and urgency, I start to reach for the truck keys. I'm ready to go right now and find it. I stop myself though, realizing that no matter how much I want to get to it as soon as possible, I have to be really careful. It's already nearly four thirty. Mom will be home in another hour or two and I would never even make it there before dark. It's been years since I walked those vague trails and there aren't any houses for miles. I would be sure to get lost. I've got to be smart about this.

Tomorrow morning we'll go. Tonight, when Chris calls, I'll fill him in and we can meet early in the morning. "Thanks, Jake. I'll have to sneak out there tomorrow during the day. I'm sorry I didn't tell you about it right away. I promise to tell you what I find though." I focus my attention back on my brother, thankful for his help.

"I'm not a baby anymore you know," he says quietly.

"I know you aren't, Jake. I'm sorry if I treat you like one." I mean it, too. He hugs me again, accepting my apology and then asks what's for dinner.

Grateful for the distraction, I get out all the ingredients to make spaghetti. It's one of the other few dishes I can manage. Looking at the clock, my stomach knots up again as I realize I'll have to face my mom soon. I start moving faster, hoping to be done and hidden away in our rooms long before she gets here.

SEVENTEEN

Friday morning comes quickly. Rolling out of bed, I am both excited to finally be *doing* something but scared at the same time.

Chris called me last night like he had promised, but we were only able to talk briefly in whispered conversation. Sitting in my closet, I told him Jake had figured it out and we needed to meet up early to go for a long hike. I was hesitant to give too many details over the phone, his paranoia rubbing off on me.

Chris immediately pointed out the big flaws in my plan. Both of our mothers weren't leaving for work until around eight a.m. so if we failed to show up at school and they called, our bluff would be up, and we'd be out of time. I feel like it's already borrowed. It's becoming obvious that we're going to have to leave and it'll most likely be this weekend. I don't know what will happen to Jake or us if we stay, but I'm not willing to hang around and find out. Before we leave though, we need to get to the duck blind, contact as many other non-Shiners as we can, and of course come up with a plan on where we're going to go.

One possibility is an old hunting cabin Dad took us to a few times that usually sits vacant. I'm not even sure who owns it, or if it's still standing. It's in the middle of nowhere deep in the Cascades and not many people know about it. There's a creek nearby with fresh water and a big fireplace in the main room. Both Jake and I can hunt and fish so I think we could at least ride out the summer months there if we need to.

I reluctantly agreed with Chris to wait until after school. One more day of trying to carry out this charade, but it's necessary. We can't run now. If what we find at the duck blind leads us back to my house, and something in my dad's possessions, we'll need access to it. Never mind the fact that Jacob will be at home and we can't take any chances with him either. Just one more day.

I remind myself of this, as I get ready for school. Emerging from my room, I can hear sounds in the kitchen and assume that Mom is already up. She came home last night when she had said she would, and we were already in our rooms. Turned out I didn't need to worry about avoiding her. She pretty much went straight to her own room, stopping only long enough to tell me she would be going back to work at eight this morning. Her TV turned on, the bath water ran in her bathroom for a while, and she never came back out.

I'm pretty sure she knows I never really got sick, but

for whatever reason isn't calling me on it yet. I have a feeling that she's waiting for something and I want to make sure I'm long gone before it happens. I don't know if she believes Jacob. Maybe.

Sneaking into his room now, I gently shake him awake. He looks at me sleepily and then startles awake. "What's wrong?" he gasps, looking wide-eyed at the door, like one of the aliens from his video games is about to come crashing through.

"Nothing Jake, I'm sorry if I scared you. I just want to let you know that I'm leaving for school. Chris and I decided to wait until later to go to the duck blind; we have to be careful not to get anyone suspicious. Did Mom say anything to you last night?"

Shaking his head, he lays back down, obviously relieved. "Nah. She poked her head in and stood there for a while, but I pretended to be asleep. Even made sure my breathing was really slow and stuff. She finally left. Is she gone yet?"

"No. She's in the kitchen. But she said she has work at eight so she should be leaving in less than an hour. Will you be okay? Can you pretend to still be asleep?" I ask him, feeling now like this wasn't such a good idea.

"I'm fine," he says reassuringly. "I have Baxter. Will you leave him in here instead of putting him out back? Please?" Baxter raises his head at the sound of his name and looks at me challengingly, daring me to even suggest it.

"Of course he can stay in here," I tell him, patting Baxter. He chuffs at me approvingly and then stretches, spreading out the whole width of the bed. Tucking Jacob back in, I put a finger to my lips as I back out and silently close the door.

Mom is sitting at the kitchen table eating a bowl of oatmeal, and watches me solemnly as I grab a bag of pop tarts and get my backpack. "See you later," I say neutrally, opening the garage door. I don't look back, knowing that she is still studying me. I have no desire to look into those cold, dark eyes again.

I meet Chris at our spot before class but we keep it brief. Everyone is behaving more and more like a hive mind. We don't think they can actually read minds or anything, or else we would be in big trouble. It's more like an ant or bee colony. They seem to have a collective conscious and any behavior outside the normal routine is sure to bring unwanted attention.

We must walk in an orderly fashion without talking or looking around, go straight to our assigned seats and take out our assigned material and begin studying. When the bell rings, everyone stands together and leaves in the same order. Everything that is done, every motion or look or gesture is with a purpose. It is all extremely efficient and sterile, without emotion or individual thought. It's just plain creepy.

We agree to watch for any of the kids taken from the gym yesterday and then follow our plan later to look them up and find out where they live. We'll meet after school at the end of the main hiking trail I told him about. We figure it's best to go separately so we're less likely to be seen together.

It doesn't take long before I get an idea as to what happened to some of my classmates that were taken. In first period, Tim and Matt obviously weren't Shiners yesterday. Tim is now gone, but Matt is slumped in his desk, quite sick. It's the same in the rest of my classes too. I estimate about half of the kids from the gym are gone, so around fifty. The rest of them are here, but sick. The small list of names I had from yesterday is shrinking. Their symptoms aren't horrible, but definitely more pronounced than Mom's were the day after the meteor shower. It makes me wonder what was done to them. It makes me nervous.

A sense of urgency builds throughout the day and I find it really hard to sit still in my last period. Time is running out. They've found a way to infect those of us that were initially immune to the virus. They are turning us all into Shiners. We have to get away.

I fight back the rising panic and almost run from the building at the end of the school day. Hurrying to my truck, I lock myself inside and take long slow breaths while listening to some music. After a couple of minutes, I take out my cell phone and call home. When Jacob answers on the fourth ring, I almost cry with relief and ask him if everything is all right there, and if Mom went to work. Yes, things are fine and yes, she went to work. He sounds so relaxed that it's tempting to believe this is all a dream, but I know better than to fall into that trap.

It only takes me ten minutes to drive out to the trailhead. The small parking lot is empty so I pick a spot and get the other backpack I had put in the backseat last night. It's got water, snacks, and my good hiking shoes in it. Putting the shoes on, I sling the bag over my shoulder and set out at a brisk pace. It will take close to two hours to reach the blind so I'll be getting back home barely an hour before Mom does. I have to make this fast.

A mile up the main trail, over half way to the end of it I look up at the blazing sun and notice a column of dark grey smoke off to the left. That's odd.

While I catch my breath and take a drink of water, I wonder at what it could be. It's too dark for wood smoke and there aren't any houses out this way. As I watch, the column thickens and the hairs on the back of my neck start to stand up. Shifting back and forth on my feet, I debate whether to wait here for Chris or take ten minutes to go investigate.

We had agreed to meet at the end of this trail, and he was going to start out about ten minutes or so after me. We decided to leave our phones in our cars, just in case the GPS in them can be tracked. Not much of a signal out here anyway. After a slight hesitation, I step away from the path and head into the heavy woods.

The only other thing out this way is the old City Dump. It hasn't been in use for two years, ever since they built the nice new one on the other end of town. If I'm right, it should be right over the next little rise, a couple hundred yards away.

In only a few minutes, I reach the top of a long slope, and spread out below me is a narrow, green valley. At the bottom, about a football field length away, are the remains of the dump. What should be an abandoned field surrounded by old barbed wire fencing, is instead full of activity.

Instinct tells me to stay hidden and I listen to it without hesitation. Dropping down to my stomach, I hide behind some shrubs and peak out cautiously, squinting to make sense of the scene below me.

In the middle is what looks to be a freshly dug pit, the bulldozer still idling alongside the far edge of it. The smoke I saw is rising from this hole and a gray haze has settled over the small valley.

Several pick-up trucks and a couple of long white vans are scattered around the field. I recognize them as city vehicles and I wonder if maybe they started using this site again for whatever reason. A handful of people are milling about, and it looks like there's a bunch of garbage or bags piled up in the hole.

As I watch, two men walk up to the edge, carrying something between them. With some effort, they toss it into the pit and then walk back to one of the vans that sits idling with its back doors open.

In a minute or two, they are back again, this time with a lighter load. My brain can't quite wrap itself around the image, and I'm struggling to understand what I'm seeing. Then, as they swing their arms back, readying to toss it in, I recognize the tie-dyed shirt that Heather had been wearing yesterday at school. I'd thought it was rather bold, because in the center of all the random color was a great big yellow smiley face and the words "because I can" written under it. That same smiley face now flashes at me as it flies through the air ... as *she* flies through the air on her way to the bottom of the pit. Her long brown hair flows out as her body rolls a couple of times, coming to rest up against Tim in his distinctive, bright blue and white letterman jacket.

Vomit rising in my throat, I scramble away from the edge, away from the horror going on down there. Slapping both my hands over my mouth, I'm desperate to muffle the scream that I know is about to escape. Looking around at this suddenly alien landscape, I try to figure out which way to go but in my panic, I've become disoriented.

Stumbling a couple of steps backwards down the slope, I happen to look to my left and catch a glimpse of Chris huddled behind some trees not more than a hundred feet away from me. He must have seen the smoke too and gone to investigate the same as me. His face is pale and he's looking at me wild eyed, his finger raised to his mouth, the other hand gesturing urgently to me to get down.

With a tunnel vision brought on by my terror, I focus on his hand and follow its command, dropping down on all fours. Once on the ground, I lose sight of him, and stare momentarily at the leaves under my hands, my heartbeat pounding in my head, filling my world.

Then something in me snaps and I'm scrambling frantically on my hands and knees down the hill, whimpering as I go. Nearing where I left the trail, I slide sideways into a hollow and roll the rest of the way to the bottom. Curling into a ball at the base of a tree, I put my hands over my ears, trying to block out a wailing sound that surrounds me and won't stop.

I become aware of hands gripping my arms and fight to get away, kicking and screaming. "Alex!" Chris yells, and his voice breaks through my blind panic as he wrestles with me there in the pine needles and leaves. "Alex!" he yells again, his own emotions making his voice thick but still recognizable.

I finally calm down enough to realize that the wailing is coming from me, and that I must stop. I have to stop. Reaching out frantically, I cling to Chris's shirt and bury my face in his broad chest. His hands go to my back and he rocks me slowly, murmuring into my hair much the same way I did to Jacob that night we were told that Dad had died.

Through the haze of fear, I'm aware that we are in a dangerous situation and as much as I want to have a complete breakdown, I can't. Not if I want to survive, not if I want my brother to survive. I will *not* let him end up in that pit!

That thought brings me around and I pull away from Chris, gasping at the sharp contrast of emotions raging through me. Now I'm mad. So mad I could spit, or hit something or start yelling again. Instead, I sit on my knees and look intensely at his face. I imagine mine looks similar; much older than our sixteen and seventeen years ... and determined.

"They killed them, Chris," I whisper hoarsely, my hands balling into fists. "Heather, Tim, I think I saw your friend Kevin ... *down* there. There has to be over two hundred bodies. Why? Why would they do that? Kids from school, people from town. Because they didn't get sick, didn't change into Shiners? I don't understand."

"I know, Alex. You're right. It's beyond understanding. They're gone, and we can't help them now," he says, gesturing back towards the dump. "But we might be able to help millions of others. If there's a way to stop this before it spreads, we have to do everything possible."

"We *have* to stop them," I say with desperation.

"Then let's go," he says, pulling me to my feet.

As we stumble back out onto the trail, I struggle to regain the strength in my legs, which are threatening to turn to jelly. Chris takes my hand in his and leads the way, holding on tight. As we push ahead, I look up again at the rising smoke … the ashes of our friends.

EIGHTEEN

We walk in stunned silence until we reach the end of the marked trail. My tears have dried but anger burns hot in my chest, pushing me on. When we're done here, I plan on making an anonymous call to 911. I don't care what the risks are. We have to try to let people know what's happening. I move ahead past a "No Trespassing, Private Property" sign, and briefly survey the overgrown game trails. "This way," I say sharply, pointing to our left.

As we trudge through the long grass growing stubbornly in the gaps between the evergreens, Chris moves up alongside me. "Alex, I've been thinking about the numbers involved in all of this."

I look sideways at him, not sure what he means. "What numbers?"

"The earth's population is roughly seven billion. If your friend on that message board was right and this virus targets our DNA based on purity, then we can assume the

U.S. is going to have one of the highest infection rates. It has one of the most diverse populations in the world and inner-racial births. So if we drop it down from eighty percent to seventy percent for worldwide infection, that gives us almost five billion initially infected. We're basically ground zero though. It seems like it took about four days for it to spread to the East Coast of the States and I would think the rest of the world is one to two weeks behind them. That means we can assume the Shiners will be infecting those left and then killing anyone who's immune everywhere else too, but we have a little time."

The full meaning of what he's just said slowly seeps in and I stop. Chris takes a few steps before he realizes I'm no longer beside him. Looking back at me, he must see the knowledge of his statement in my eyes because he immediately looks regretful and doubles back.

"No," I say, putting out a hand to stop him, walking backwards into a tree. "No. You can't be right. I'm not very good at math, but even I can figure out what half of two billion is."

Ignoring my pleas, he steps in front of me and takes me by the shoulders. "Maybe I *am* wrong Alex. There could be others out there that know more than we do and are trying to stop this right now, too. We can't count on that though. The bodies in that pit, as horrible as it is, are *nothing* compared to what could happen if this isn't stopped."

Seeing the truth in his eyes, I close my own against it. Taking a deep breath, I draw strength again from the fire burning in me and for the first time in over a year, say a silent prayer; *God, please … please, if you can hear me, give me the strength I need for this. I can't do it by myself. Please help me.*

Feeling a sense of peace and resolve that defies explanation, I push away from the tree. "We need to keep moving then," I say to Chris, confidently meeting his gaze. I see a mixture of grief, compassion and something I can't quite define before he lets go of my arms and turns away.

Looking up at the sun that's now making its way to the horizon, he starts off at a brisk pace, almost jogging. I do my best to keep up. Within fifteen minutes, we emerge through some foliage and find ourselves on the edge of a large marshy area, full of cattails and frogs.

"It's not much farther," I tell him, turning right and walking along with the shoreline on our left. There is no trail now, just the water to guide me. The familiar smell of moss and pond water surrounds us and I know we're close.

Hopefully nothing has happened to our secret hunting spot, and my pulse quickens at the thought. Any number of things might have destroyed it, from falling trees to rising waters or vandals. Just when I've convinced myself that all I'll find is wreckage, I catch sight of a distinct structure. "There it is!" I shout, excited.

Running the rest of the way, tripping over roots and scratched by vines, I finally reach the duck blind. Seeing it brings back a rush of emotions and tears start falling before I can stop them. Kneeling down in the dirt, I reach out and run my hand over the smooth boards that line the floor of the three-sided enclosure. Its partial roof barely qualifies as one, and is covered by a camouflage net that is tattered and faded, tendrils of fabric flapping in the slight breeze. The walls however are solid, its posts set deep into the soft ground.

When we would come here to hunt, there was just enough room for all three of us to sit inside, and then Dad would pull the netting down to cover the open backside, sort of like a tent. There are three small window-like openings in the front, water-facing side. We would lean our rifles through them and wait for the ducks to come in. It was a good spot, and Dad had been very proud of it.

Looking at it now, I begin to scrutinize it in a different way. I hadn't given much thought as to where something might be hidden. I find myself anxious again at the realization that we might not find it. I look around at the lowering sun and start urgently running my hands over the boards of the floor.

"The last hieroglyph was burial," Chris says, kneeling down beside me. "Do you think it might be under the floor? Maybe we should start pulling up the boards."

I'm about to agree with him when I reach the far left corner and my fingers encounter something different in the wood. Leaning my face down closer, I squint to see in the murky light. "Do you have a flashlight?" I ask Chris, "I forgot to bring one."

Digging around in his backpack, he comes up with one and hands it to me. Shining it in the corner, my heart races again, but this time in excitement. Etched clearly, deeply into the floorboard is the picture of the vulture. I turn to look at Chris, and he already has a large screwdriver in his hand. I move aside and he quickly wedges it under the edge of the plank and pries it up. The wood protests only briefly and gives way with a loud pop. Chris crawls back and I shine the flashlight into the space that was under it.

"There's something there! Hurry Chris, pull off another plank." I slide over again as he pulls off the next board, and then another one. Underneath is a large space nearly filled by a big burlap sack, over a foot in diameter.

Reaching down, I try to lift it up and find that I can't. It's too heavy. I let Chris take a shot at it and with some effort, he works it out of the tight space and up onto the floor.

Sitting there, we look at each other, the bag between us. So much depends on what's inside. Now that the time is here I'm afraid of finding out that there's nothing we can do about the infection. "Open it," Chris says quietly, and I draw confidence from him.

I untie the cord wrapped around the top of the sack. As the knot slips off, the cloth drops down, revealing something that looks like a metallic box, shrink wrapped inside a thick, black plastic. I was expecting something old or ancient looking, like everything else has been up until now, so I'm surprised by it. Reaching out, I unzip the plastic, breaking the seal. As the shrink-wrap expands, releasing its grip on the box, I look at the darkening woods behind us, paranoid that we aren't alone. I quickly pull the plastic off, eager to get this done

157

and get back home to Jacob.

The large box is a foot tall and long, with no obvious way to open it. It looks like one of those fire safes and I know Dad kept something similar in the back of the closet in his office. I've seen inside that one several times though, including before his funeral to retrieve his will. That one opens with a key, but I don't see a key hole anywhere on this. Imbedded in the top is a three-inch square black screen, with what looks like one small button. I push it, and a blue grid lights up across the screen. I look up at Chris, unsure of what to do next.

He's studying it, his face dark in the gathering shadows. "Put your thumb on it," he says finally.

The screen has gone dark, so I push the button again, and this time when it lights up, I place my right thumb in the middle of the grid. At first, nothing happens, but then there is a slight mechanical, whirring sound and a click as the lock on the lid is released. "How …"

"He was your dad," Chris interrupts. "He could have gotten your print from any number of things.

Not wanting to waste any time discussing it, I open the lid and look inside. There is a purple velvet sack, like what you expect to find precious jewels in, holding something large and round. Reaching in, I pick it up. It's slightly smaller than a bowling ball, but just as heavy. Perplexed, I awkwardly remove the velvet as I hold it against my body and am so unprepared for what I see that I almost drop it.

Staring up at me is a perfectly carved skull out of what appears to be crystal. I look at Chris, mouth open, and to my amazement, he starts to laugh.

"Are you serious?" he says, reaching out for the carving. "A crystal skull? Just when you think it can't get any weirder."

Handing it over to him, I watch as he holds it up, examining it. Having been a member to one of the biggest conspiracy theory websites, I am of course familiar with the legendary crystal skulls. Thirteen of them have been found in different parts of the world and some believe them to be anywhere from 5,000 to more than 30,000 years old. Others think they are a hoax, but the jury is still out.

There is actually quite a following for some of the different theories, including the lost civilization of Atlantis, or that they stem from some super ancient society and are computers. I can't believe that I am looking at what seems to either be one, or a great copy of one. The only difference that I can see is that on the forehead there is a carving of a pyramid, with rays coming out from it, very similar to the carving on the medallion. I reach subconsciously for the weight at my neck, touching it through my shirt to assure me it's still there.

"You know about the whole crystal skull thing?" I ask Chris as he stands up, cradling the skull in his arm.

"Sure I do. I've read a lot about it. There are even some Native American legends surrounding them," he explains as he steps out of the blind and into the fading light of the day. Holding it out to get a better look at it, the sun hits it, and we both marvel at the display of prisms reflected through it. So it's definitely quartz crystal.

Going off instinct, I take the skull from Chris and with some effort, hold it so that the thin rays of sunlight hit the statue at the base of the skull. As it begins to glow, I see that the intricate surface carving is redirecting the light, bouncing it off the many angles until it comes out the front of the carved pyramid in a solid beam.

Realizing my head is in the way of the beam, I move it to the side and then follow the light, almost dropping the crystal again. Chris gasps in surprise and moves in closer. Projected into the shadows of the trees, hovering in the air almost like a holograph, the prismatic light isn't scattered, but cleverly constructed to form an elaborate design.

"That's a double helix," he almost whispers, in awe. "A strand of DNA."

I knew it had looked familiar, but now that Chris states the obvious, I'm overwhelmed by the implications. Unable to hold it up any longer, I lower the skull and watch as the blueprint for human design fades away. What right does that have to be doing inside an artifact that could possibly be thousands of years old? I look down at it, not sure if it's good or bad. Since it was from my father, I decide not to throw it like the bowling ball it reminds me of.

Setting it down carefully on the soft ground, I go back to the box and look inside, seriously hoping to find some sort of an explanation or directions. In the bottom of the box is a single piece of folded parchment paper. In the center, holding the sides closed is a very formal looking glob of red wax, the impression of the medallion carving clearly in the middle of it.

Lifting it out, I wave it towards Chris. "Looks like you were right," I tell him as he comes to sit next to me. "It must have been my dad's personal seal or something." A sense of urgency is pushing at me and I almost rip the paper as I try to open it faster than the wax will allow.

Inside I find my dad's unique script and my hopes rise as I start to read it out loud:

Alexis,

I knew you would find it! I'm sure at this point you'll have more questions than I'm able to answer, but in case this is found by anyone other than you, I have to limit what I say. I know by now you'll appreciate that. If the anti-virus were to fall into the hands of our adversaries, the damage they would unleash is almost as bad as the virus itself.

It's critical that you find Professor Alim Hassan. He would have been sent to replace me after my death and would have been in contact with you. You should know where he is.

Go to him. Take the skull. He will be able to answer all your questions and explain what it is you need to do. Then you must go to the cabin and let its warmth guide you. Do not trust anyone else.

You are now part of the "Khufu Bast," or the "Pyramid Protectors." It is your heritage, your bloodline. The medallion is the Mubarak family seal, passed on for 5,000 years to the first-born son, but now to my first-born daughter. The knowledge is sacred and protected, Alexis. Show this seal to Professor Hassan and he will know that you can now be entrusted with the information necessary to stop the spreading evil.

It is a plague from an unknown world, maybe even the devil himself, sent to steal our free will and prepare us for servitude. We have risen against it before and with God's help will do it again. Do not lose faith, Alex. I love you-
Dad

Silence hangs between us for a couple of minutes. Finally, I re-fold the paper and put in the pocket of my backpack. I look at Chris then, and am encouraged to see him gathering all our things with purpose, the despair so obvious before now replaced by hope.

Setting the safe back under the floorboards, he slides the skull into its bag and places it in his backpack. Lifting it up onto his shoulders, he then reaches out a hand to me. I take it and he pulls me to my feet.

"We have to get back to Jacob as fast as possible," I say to him, already headed back the way we came. "We're leaving. Tonight."

"You know where this professor is?" he asks as we trot along the edge of the murky water, sensing that I'm not ready to talk about the note.

"Yes. He's the one that called the other day; I remember now where I've heard that voice. He's the same man that was at Dad's funeral and gave us Baxter as a gift. He came over a few more times afterwards and had dinner with us once. I thought he was weird though and caught him snooping in Dad's office. He said he and Dad were childhood friends and taught at the University together. After Dad moved here the professor went on to get his PhD in biology, genetics I think. Says he doesn't like to be called doctor because he will always be a teacher. I've never been to his house, but I know where it is." Almost falling over a stump, I catch myself and then run to catch up with Chris.

As we turn onto the game trail, I see that the sun is almost below the tree line now and my newfound hope gives way to fear. Mom will be home soon and I know with certainty that my little brother is in danger. I should have never left him alone. I begin to run and pass Chris, my legs carried by desperation.

NINETEEN

The ride home is torture. An overwhelming need to get to Jacob has grabbed me and won't let go. I'm already driving ten over the speed limit and it takes all my will to keep from going faster. We can't take the risk of being pulled over, not now. It's safe to assume that most, if not all of the police force are Shiners. I still plan on calling the authorities, but after I have Jake and know that he's safe.

Chris is sitting silently beside me. We left his car back at the parking lot. We would be coming back this way to go to the professor's house, and I have more gas than he does. No sense taking both vehicles.

We haven't said much since leaving the woods. In a way, I'm grateful. This is taking me awhile to make sense of. I am thinking of the other people in my life that I love, in addition to my mom and brother. I'm actually relieved now that Missy and my grandparents were sick.

At least I don't have to worry about them being killed. Glancing in the rearview mirror, I speed up just a bit more.

"He used the word 'anti-virus,' " Chris says next to me, making me jump.

Thinking back over the message, I try to remember what it said. "Something about it falling into the hands of our adversaries, that it would almost do as much damage as the virus?" I ask.

"Yes, pretty much. When I read up on the viruses, they talked about reverse-engineering. If you can isolate the genetic material, you can use it, manipulate it. Can you imagine what someone could do with this virus?" He looks at me from the passenger seat, and I marvel at his ability to see the bigger picture. All I can focus on right now is getting around the next curve, and he's thinking about reverse engineering a virus. Amazing.

"I don't know, Chris. Honestly, I'm not looking that far ahead right now. I guess that might explain though why this is all so secretive. Obviously, the Khufu Bast is a secret society, and there is at least one other group trying to find whatever it is they have. Why didn't he just tell me though? Or at least leave something a bit more obvious behind that I would find sooner so we could have prevented all of this?"

"It wouldn't have been safe to do it before the meteor shower," Chris suggests.

"What do you mean?" I ask, still not getting it.

"They killed your dad, Alex. They obviously knew about the virus, and that your dad had access to this anti-virus. I'm thinking that whatever he's leading us to is a critical link in stopping the infection, and whoever killed him did so to keep that knowledge from getting out. They would have been watching you. Waiting for you to lead them to it." That thought creeps me out a bit, and I wonder if he might be right.

"I'll bet you that they were well prepared to escape before the Holocene shower," he continues. "I think they want to use it, not be controlled by it. They'll probably lay low until the initial phase is over. Once all the symptoms of this "flu" are gone, the carriers won't be contagious by the air-borne method anymore. It'll only be blood borne."

"What if they aren't in hiding, and are still watching me?" I ask, looking in the mirror again. To my relief, I don't see any headlights behind us.

"They would have done something by now, Alex. Probably would have right away."

Not liking the idea of my father's killers stalking me, I have to accept the fact that I can't do anything about it right now. My anxiety amplified, we turn the corner onto our block, and as I push the garage door opener, I know immediately that something is wrong.

Just ahead, sitting in our driveway are two strange cars. Chris and I exchange a knowing look and I hit the accelerator. My truck jumps the curb and I come to a screeching halt halfway in the garage, the door still slowly rising.

Leaping down, I'm met by frantic barking coming from in front of the truck. As I run for the door leading into the kitchen, I pass Baxter. He's tied up to a workbench, foaming at the mouth. I don't have time to set him free because coming from inside the house is a sound I've prayed to never hear.

My little brother, the one I promised to protect, is screaming. Not the kind that means he is hurt or mad, but the blood curdling kind born from the terror of death.

My vision again narrowing, I am vaguely aware that I am inside the house and flying down the hallway. Time slows down and my hearing actually recedes, as I get closer to his room. His door is slightly ajar, the light spilling out. As I come up on my dad's office, I veer inside and without even thinking, grab the loaded service revolver from the duty belt hanging next to the desk. Dad had taught me how to work the double release on the holster and I press the levers with ease. Holding it at the ready, I brush past Chris on my way back out the door, not even acknowledging him.

Quickly crossing the hallway, I hit Jake's door with my shoulder as I slam a bullet into the chamber. Raising the weapon, I take in the nightmarish seen before me. Two men that I have never seen before are on either side of Jacob's bed, holding down his arms and legs. Mom is standing at his side, her back to me, holding a syringe over his bared arm.

My head is filled with my brother's screams. His body is writhing on the bed, the covers kicked off and scattered on the floor. "Stop it!" I yell, my voice sounding far away. "Stop it, Mom!"

I have the gun pointed at her back only a few feet

away … but I can't pull the trigger. I can't shoot her. Before I can determine if he's been injected or not, she turns on me. With a speed that isn't human, the gun is knocked from my hand. I'm propelled through the air and slammed into the wall behind me, her fingers at my throat.

Her face is inches from my own as I begin to black out; the pressure against my carotid arteries cutting off the blood to my brain. Frantically pulling at her wrist, I see the syringe raised above me in her other hand and look in her eyes one last time. Shimmering slightly, there is only a casual curiosity at my anguish.

As the edges of my vision fade away, she suddenly begins to contort violently. My neck is released and her face pulls into a hideous grimace as she falls backwards onto the floor. Standing behind her is Chris, my dad's Taser in one hand, the fallen gun picked up and in the other. Two copper wires lead from the Taser and into my mom's back.

Turning from me, he confronts the guys advancing on him and unlike me, shoots without hesitation. Several shots explode in the room and the percussion breaks through my paralysis.

I fall to my knees, rubbing at my throat, struggling to regain control over my body. "Alex!" Chris is in my face, yelling at me. "Alex, did she expose you?" Concentrating on his eyes, his nice, normal eyes, I swim to the surface of my consciousness and my surroundings start to come back into focus.

"Alex!" he shouts again, and I slowly stand back up

with his help.

"I'm okay," I gasp, trying to push past him. "I'm okay; she didn't inject me with anything. Jacob!" He finally releases me and I stumble over Mom's writhing body and towards the bed. Jake is curled into a ball, moaning.

One of the men is lying on the floor at the foot of the bed, holding his stomach and making strange, gurgling sounds. The other one is sprawled across the top of the partially exposed mattress, face down and not moving. Blood is rapidly spreading out into the foam from under him.

Chris hands me the Taser and scoops Jacob up in one swooping motion. As we reach the door, the electricity stops flowing and Mom's body becomes still, her breathing loud and rapid. Pressing the trigger, I wince slightly as she begins seizing again. I can't take a chance that she'll recover faster than normal. I drop the device and step out of the room.

Chris is already disappearing outside through the kitchen door. Breathing hoarsely, I run back to Dad's office and grab my rifle off the gun rack. Pulling out the top drawer of his desk, I take a set of keys and open the only locked cabinet. Quickly selecting two boxes of ammo, I race back down the hallway, the sound of the crackling Taser following me.

Once in the garage, I pause long enough to untie Baxter from his leash and we both scramble into the backseat of the running truck, where Jake is. Before I even have the door closed, Chris is backing out of the driveway recklessly, taking out our mailbox, and clipping the bumper of one of the other cars.

"I'm sorry, Jacob," I whisper, pulling him into my lap. "I'm so sorry I left you. I should have never left you."

Tears fall from me uncontrollably and I sob out the last words. Struggling to wipe the damp hair from his face, I cup his cheeks with both of my hands. Forcing him to look at me, I search his face for answers.

Tires screeching, we fly around a corner and then back onto the road that leads out of town. Chris turns on the headlights to push back the night and we accelerate up the country road.

"Are you okay, Jake?" I beg, desperately wanting him to smile and just be my silly little brother again. To go back in time to the day we were sitting around our fishing hole, unaware of anything so evil and terrifying.

But he just stares at me, eyes wide and full of knowledge a boy his age shouldn't have. In answer, he simply holds his left arm out in front of me. Looking down, my breath catches. Panic claws at my throat and robs me of any encouraging words

A small line of blood trickles out from a puncture wound in the crook of his arm. Baxter whines softly and pushes his way onto both our laps, sniffing at it. I pull the sleeve down on his Batman pajamas, covering the small wound, trying to hide the reality. I can't help but think of a word used by my dad in his letter. It's our bloodline. I close my eyes against the image and gather Jacob close.

TWENTY

The professor's house is a large estate several miles outside of town. I call out a direction to Chris every once in awhile, but it only involves a few turns. Most of my energy is spent trying to keep my composure for Jacob's sake. I'm glad that he is at least talking now, but I'm having a hard time answering his questions.

"Why did she do that?" Is the first thing out of his mouth, and probably the most difficult to address. "Who were those guys? Why was she with them?"

"Shhh," I tell him, when he begins to cry. "I'm not sure, Jake. Mom isn't herself right now, you know. This virus is making people do really weird things. It's okay though, they can't hurt you anymore. I won't let them." My guilt is almost too much to cope with, but I push back the rising black tide and focus on what is important. We have to make it through this and then we'll deal with everything else.

"What was in the shot?" he demands, rubbing at his arm. "Was it medicine? Why wouldn't she tell me what they were doing? She *hurt* me, Alex!"

I'm pretty sure that there was blood in the syringe, probably her own. I didn't stop to examine it, but that's what it looked like and it would make sense based on Chris's theory about secondary infections. But I can't tell Jacob that.

"I don't know, Jake," I lie. Well, it's a half-truth, because I can't be sure, and he's had enough trauma for one night. There's no way I'm telling him what it most likely was. In fact, I don't think *I'm* ready to accept it either, that my little brother could be lost to me too.

"Hey! Were those guys *dead?*" he says abruptly, sitting up straight. "Did Chris kill them? Won't he get in trouble?"

"No, he isn't in trouble," I say calmly. "He was protecting us, Jake. We're going to go see Professor Hassan now. You know, the guy that gave you Baxter? Dad left me a note that he wrote before he died, that said the professor would know what to do to help make people get better. He used to be Dad's friend." I'm hoping he won't notice I didn't answer the first part of his question.

When I look back down at him however, I see that he has a dazed look and his eyelids are growing heavy. The shock of it all is taking its toll. Sleep might be the best thing that could happen to him right now anyway, so I pull him in a bit closer and try to keep him warm. By the time we reach the estate ten minutes later, he is sound asleep. I envy his ability to escape this living nightmare.

Before Chris turns off the main road, I check out the back window to make sure there's no sign of headlights behind us. We drive up a long, winding driveway that's lined on either side by tall oak trees. Pulling into a large parking area, I look up at a beautiful, A-frame log house. Green lawn spreads away from it, ending at the darkening woods in the distance.

Chris comes around and opens the back door. Silently, he reaches inside and effortlessly picks up Jake. As he takes him from me, I stop him with a hand on his wrist. "You didn't have a choice," is all I say. Pausing, he finally looks at me and I can see the turmoil he's feeling inside.

"Can you carry the backpack?" he asks, clearly not wanting to discuss the shooting.

I pick up the heavy bag in response and drop down off the seat and onto the ground behind them. The sun is well below the horizon now, and night is setting in. The windows in the house glow warmly, confirming the impression I've built up about it as a place of refuge and protection. Now that we are finally here, I hope that we can get some answers and maybe even a few hours of sleep.

As we walk across the wide front porch and I ring the bell, I can imagine how we must look, the three of us huddled there with Baxter sitting at our feet. The door is opened almost immediately and I recognize the pudgy, middle-aged man as the same one that came the day of Dad's funeral. He had introduced himself as an old family friend from Egypt and we had never even thought to question it. When he moved into town later that year, he invited me out here for a visit but I never took him up on it. He's barely taller than me, with short salt and pepper hair and a pointed beard. The graying hair on his face stands out in stark contrast to his bronze Egyptian skin. He stares at us down his hooked nose, over his glasses and looks as if he isn't that happy to see us.

To my surprise, instead of inviting us inside or asking why we are here, he simply kneels down in front of Baxter. Grabbing him behind the ears, he holds his face close to his own and looks intensely into his eyes.

"Baxter, old friend! It is a pleasure to see you again." Baxter chuffs at him politely, but rather than licking him like I would expect, he gently pulls his head away and sits back on his haunches, watching the professor.

Chuckling, he slowly stands back up and finally addresses us. "Well, what are you doing just standing there? Come in, come in!" Chris and I glance at each other and then follow our odd host inside.

The main part of the cabin is all open and includes the dining room, kitchen, and a huge stone fireplace in the family room. Towering ceilings make space for the wall of windows on the front of the house that I'm sure give an amazing view in the daytime.

There is a large fire roaring and I'm finding it a bit warm, despite the cool air of the spring night. Limping slightly, Professor Hassan directs Chris to lay Jacob on the only couch in the large room. Jake stirs slightly, but with the light of the fire warming his face, he settles back down and doesn't wake up.

We go and sit around a big wooden table on the opposite side of the room so we can talk without disturbing him. A gigantic cat is perched on a bench near us, keeping a close eye on Baxter, who choses to lie on the floor by the couch. He in turn is watching the cat. I give him a look to let him know I've got my eye on him. He sneezes in my direction and places his head on his paws, pretending to be uninterested.

"Your mom is sick." It isn't so much a question as it is a statement. I look at the man who is supposed to give us all the answers and am not sure how I feel about him.

"Yes. She got the flu last Saturday. Actually, I think it started Friday night, right after the shower," I explain. Not sure what to do with the heavy backpack, I consider taking the skull out now, but instead set it carefully on the floor next to my chair.

Nodding, he pushes back from the table and stands up again, rubbing his hands together and muttering quietly to himself. He seems agitated all of a sudden and unable to sit still. "*Now* you decide to come. Not this morning, not last night but *now*." He's looking at me somewhat accusingly and I don't know what I'm supposed to say.

"We just found the directions to come see you," Chris says, his tone cautious. "We had no idea until this afternoon that you had anything to do with all of ... *this.*"

"Of course, of course," he says quickly. "I'm sure you came as soon as you knew." Seeming to accept the explanation, he sits back down and places both his hands on the table. "Now! I believe you have something to show me before we discuss anything further." He looks at me expectantly, eyebrows raised.

At first, I just stare blankly at him. Chris nudges me and points to my neck. "Oh!" I gasp, feeling stupid. Reaching inside my t-shirt, I pull out the seal and hold it out for the professor to see.

Pulling his glasses further down his nose, he studies the wooden carving for almost a full minute. "Excellent! I knew Adam would have made the proper arrangements. Your father was a very smart man, you know. I had hoped that I would have seen you much sooner however. You're a bit late to the game."

I am both relieved to have confirmation that we've come to the right place, but my unease is growing the longer we're here. I look to my left at Chris, and my concern is mirrored in his face.

"We came as soon as we got it figured out. It wasn't easy," I tell him slowly.

"Ah, nothing involving the Khufu Bast is easy." Removing his glasses, he spends some time cleaning them thoroughly with a large black knit scarf hanging around his neck. After replacing them, he studies me for some time. "You look just like your father, you know." He finally says, smiling broadly.

I thank him, trying to be polite but my patience is getting thin. There's no time for small talk. "I need to know what's happened," I tell him bluntly. "We know that the virus outbreak came from the Holocene meteor shower and that it's somehow changing everyone. People with purer DNA are less likely to be infected, but they've started using blood to make them sick now and are then killing anyone who is still resistant. I think my dad was involved in the Khufu Bast to somehow find an anti-virus?"

"I am sure you have many questions," he answers, leaning back in his chair and crossing his arms. "I need to start at the beginning. It is complicated." Pausing long enough to make sure he has our attention, he finally starts giving us the information we've been desperately seeking.

"Five thousand years ago that same virus was released just like it was last week, except for it started in a different location. Back then, our bloodline wasn't diluted the way it is now. Egyptians were all of Egyptian decent, and so on. Some races were more naturally immune to the disease than others were. The infection rate at that time was much less than it is today. Those that were unaffected rose up against the changed ones and after a bloody battle, defeated them. Some were kept alive and used as slaves since they were very intelligent and nimble.

"Historical records have been lost over the years and other information intentionally withheld or changed. But you need to know that there was in fact a highly technological society that existed in ancient times. Much more advanced than what we have today."

I can't believe what I'm hearing. I had scoffed at the conspiracy theories I had read about this type of thing and now wished that I'd instead spent some more time looking into it. When it's obvious we don't have any questions yet, the professor coughs slightly to clear his throat and then continues.

"The first great Egyptian pyramid is in fact a weapon. Its main purpose is to release an anti-virus that was developed after that first outbreak. A very elite society of high-ranking Egyptians was formed, called the Khufu Bast, or 'Pyramid Protectors.' Over the following thousands of years, as new races and colonies rose up on other continents, they would travel to them and share the knowledge of the pyramids with their leaders. A sentinel was then assigned to watch the pyramid, and to wait for the day of the prophesized meteor shower, to release the anti-virus. They knew that it would be during this century, but were never certain of the exact date. The Mayans thought they had it figured out, but were obviously off by a few months." He chuckles at his own joke, but stops when we don't share in his humor.

"So why didn't they just release the anti-virus on Saturday, if there are these sentinels all over the world?" Chris asks. "Aren't they still protecting the pyramids?"

Sighing, Professor Hassan taps at the table, obviously thinking about how he is going to answer. "It isn't that simple," he finally says. "You see, it's a one-shot deal. If it were to be released *before* the infection was here, it would be rendered useless. For that reason, there were certain safeguards put in place to prevent that from happening. There is one pyramid weaponized on almost every continent. Some of the knowledge has been lost over the years so we no longer understand all of the technicalities of it, but basically, they are linked together and *all* of them have to be activated before any of them release the anti-virus.

"Unfortunately, the location of the pyramid on the North American continent was lost during the small pox outbreak during the late 1700's. You have to understand that by this century, there were not that many Khufu Bast alive and only one was assigned to each location. It was months and sometimes years between communications with those remote places. That pyramid was small, had been overgrown for centuries, and was unknown to the current native tribes. By the time the sentinel's death was discovered, his body was long gone to the mountains, as well as the maps and other papers with the location of the pyramid. The only artifact recovered was the crystal skull. All we know is that it's somewhere in the Northern Cascades in what is now Washington State.

"Their whereabouts are protected with our lives and only allowed to be written in one place to prevent its discovery by anyone other than Khufu Bast. Back then, mapping techniques were still primitive. Of course, hindsight is 20/20 and I think there were many mistakes made that lead to our situation today, but they did the best they could. Amazing that any of us are left, really."

Chris excuses himself to use the bathroom and we wait for him to return. The information tumbles loosely around in my head, and I am trying my best to make sense of it. Pyramids, ancient technology and sentinels? I feel like I've stepped into the twilight zone.

Chris returns and our host looks at us expectantly. I'm not sure where to begin. "So was my dad one of the sentinels?" I might as well start there.

"Yes, yes, he was here trying to locate the pyramid. I was his replacement after he died, but had nothing to work with. He was very good at protecting our secrets. For the past two hundred years, over a dozen of us have attempted to find its position. We've been close the last ten years, but it wasn't until your dad called for a special meeting two years ago, that we finally believed it had been achieved. Without much time to spare, either."

"Why don't you use a satellite or get the government involved?" Chris asks, never failing to see the bigger picture. That would certainly make the most sense.

"The government!" The professor spits the words out as if they were foul and glares at Chris. "For the past two hundred years there has been another group forming, called the Mudameere."

"The who?" I ask, not recognizing the word. I know he is speaking Arabic, the native language of Egypt, since I had heard my dad use it before. But I don't know the language myself.

"It is Arabic, meaning *Destroyer*," he explains. "Their sole intent is to locate our secrets and twist them around to their own benefit! They have been supporting and promoting their own within numerous governments, especially the U.S. For this reason, we have been forced to retain all our ancient ways, including documentation and communication. Everything has to be completely off the grid and either written or verbal. One slip and it could all be lost, the past five thousand years of effort and hardship, all for nothing. Meanwhile, the Mudameere have embraced the new technology and used it against us. We had ten members assassinated recently, including your father."

He looks at me as he says this and my suspicions are finally confirmed. I knew my dad's death hadn't been a mugging. "Why kill him?" I ask. "If they thought he knew where the pyramid was or had special knowledge, why not just take him, and make him tell them?" Chris nods his approval at my question and I'm a little proud of myself for thinking ahead.

"They tried that before, multiple times when they first formed, with other Khufu Bast. It became obvious that we are trained early on in the art of torture and will not talk regardless of what is done. So they changed tactics. Instead of trying to unlock the final secret of how to *activate* all the pyramids, they decided to simply prevent us from *releasing* it. A goal much more easily achieved, especially since we still hadn't found the last pyramid. When they killed your father, they successfully destroyed our final hope. Or so they thought. They watched you, you know." He says while looking at me. I squirm a bit in my seat at the idea.

"That's why your dad didn't tip you off prior to the Holocene shower. He knew the Mudameere would be watching and that it would be deadly if you were caught looking for it. They, of course, have since gone into seclusion. Thousands of them escaped underground with their food rations and other essentials, days before the outbreak. They will simply wait it out and then emerge to what they think will be a new and better world. One that they can take full advantage of the benefits of this virus without the side effect of losing their free will. They have geneticists and biologists ready to isolate and manipulate the viral DNA. Imagine it, a society of highly intelligent, efficient sock puppets that they think they'll be able to control. We shall see. We shall see."

He's getting irritated again, and has begun to tap harder on the table, looking back and forth between us like he's expecting something.

"How do we activate it?" I ask hopefully, eager to get to the final point. If I'm right about my dad's last message, I know where to find the directions to the pyramid.

"Why bother?" he says loudly, his dark, bushy brows furrowed. "The Holocene virus is here. That's what the scientists are calling it now. It has spread almost everywhere. Even if the anti-virus works, the Mudameere will already have preserved samples and will eventually unleash their own kind of evil."

I know that the professor is a scientist himself and understands what he's talking about, but I find it hard to believe that he of all people would have given up. He should know more than anyone, especially as Khufu Bast, that if an anti-virus has been created before, it can be again. It doesn't make sense.

"It's quite beautiful." The change of tone in his voice causes me to look closely at him. "The virus, that is. A work of art. I've seen it, all of it. Studied it. I only had a few days with it at the lab, but even in that amount of time, I saw it for what it really is. Did you know that viruses have little bits of either DNA or RNA? Never both. There are over five thousand known viruses and most have just a few of these pieces. The Holocene virus has *hundreds* of *both*! I have been fighting to stop it my whole life. Devoted everything to it. I would have, too, if given the chance. But it's too late now."

"What if it weren't too late?" I plead, wishing he'd stop sounding like he *admires* it. "What would we have to do to release the anti-virus?" My voice has risen and my last statement comes out more like a demand than a question.

Blinking at me, he realizes how he's acting and straightens up in his chair, hands stopping their constant banging. "Well, the crystal skulls of course," he says matter-of-factly.

I start to reach for the backpack but Chris puts his hand on my arm under the table to stop my motion. I look at him questioningly and he gives a very slight shake of his head. It doesn't take a rocket scientist to figure that one out, so I keep my mouth shut about our skull.

"There is one for each designated pyramid, carefully crafted and capable of more than any other current super computer. It must be put in its proper place inside the pyramid and then activated with a small drop of blood containing the correct DNA. This will then in turn link and activate the release of all the anti-virus. If you don't even have a skull, than you're wasting your time. I don't have one and I don't know where it is." Pausing, he looks down the darkened hallway past the kitchen, tilting his head slightly as if listening.

"There's no guarantee your blood would even work," he explains, looking at me again. "You are only half Egyptian, Alex. Yours is the purest bloodline of the Khufu Bast, but we still have no way of knowing for sure."

"Your blood would work, wouldn't it?" I ask him.

"I followed your father's tradition, you know." Not grasping the change in subject, I look to where he has raised his hand to point at something.

Above the fireplace is a huge painting of him, and who I assume is his wife. They look happy together. "I met Susan right after I graduated from the University. It was love at first sight. My parents were appalled and my position in the society threatened, but I held my ground. Some things are worth fighting for."

His expression darkens when he says this and he stands again, rubbing at his arms like he's somehow cold in this hot room. "She got sick on Sunday. By the time I got back home from the city on Tuesday, she was starting to improve and I knew there was no chance for her."

"Is that who's in the room with the lock on the outside?" Chris asks evenly, and I understand now why he didn't feel comfortable sharing everything with this man. He must have seen it when he went to the bathroom.

Ignoring Chris, Professor Hassan begins to pace behind the table, starting to mutter softly under his breath again. I am beginning to fear that he is quite insane.

"I waited," he says to himself as much to us. "I waited as long as I could. You hadn't come. There was no hope. There *is* no hope. God has sent this plague on us and we must accept our fate."

"This is *not* the work of God!" Chris says fiercely, tensing in his chair.

"God has *left us!*" the professor shouts, slamming both fists down hard on the table as spittle flies from his mouth. His eyes are wild and his nostrils flared.

Baxter growls low in his throat, having come to stand beside me when he sensed the tension. I place a hand on his head to calm him, but I'm trying to guess how long it would take for me to get Jake and run out the front door.

Chris jumped up from his seat in reaction and now stands facing the professor, the table between them. "You are wrong," he says calmly, challenging him.

Laughing, the older man claps his hands together and turns away from us. "Where are my manners?" he mutters as he walks into the large, country style kitchen. "Here I have guests in my house and haven't even offered any tea! Susan would skin my hide."

Unable to keep up with his personality changes, Chris and I back away from the table and head towards the family room where Jacob is still asleep. I hold the backpack close to me, comforted by the weight of the skull.

"What kind would you like, Black or Earl Grey? Oh, are you leaving?" Walking out of the kitchen with boxes of tea in his hands, the professor seems a bit flustered and confused. I suddenly feel sorry for him. This has pushed him over the edge and I can't really blame him.

"We need ... to go," I offer.

Nodding with comprehension, he sets the boxes

down and approaches me with urgency, his face now a picture of concern. "You have a few days before they'll know everything," he says, taking one of my hands in both of his. I let him, but am not comfortable with it.

"What are you talking about?" I ask, searching his eyes for a sign of the man that was supposed to help us.

"Well, I infected myself just this afternoon so if it works, it should take a good three days before I am to the point where I will share all my knowledge with ... the Shiners."

Pulling my hand away, I take a step back from him. "Why would you do that?" I demand. "Why would you want to be one of them? They're *killing* people!"

He seems disappointed at my reaction, but takes a small step closer, pleading with me. "It probably won't work on me, but I had to try, Alex. I don't want to be alone, alone and so inadequate. It's our destiny. I knew that as soon as I saw the creation under the microscope. I'm tested as a near genius, but if this *corrects* my brain, I will be one of the smartest humans to have ever lived! Imagine what I can do, Alex! Think of all the things I can discover and create with not only that level of intelligence, but no emotional barricades!" He smiles as he's talking, getting excited at the thought of changing into one of these abominations. It's too much.

"We have to leave," I say again, moving over to the door. "Thank you for talking with us. Really. I hope that you and your wife are all right."

We make our way out into the blessedly cool air on the front porch, and Baxter runs ahead to the truck. Jake finally raises his head and looks around groggily as Chris puts him in the back seat, trying to figure out where he is.

"If you can't stop it Alex, then come back. I have a very pure, isolated virus that I can infect you with. It should work," he says encouragingly.

Appalled, I turn away from him and stumble across the driveway. I will never give up, I will never join them. I *will* finish what my father and now I am meant to do. *That* is my destiny.

TWENTY ONE

Sitting huddled on the front seat in the darkness, I stare out the window and watch the receding lights. Lights that before had represented safety but now seem to mock me, like the shining eyes of the billions of people whose only hope for a cure rests squarely on my shoulders. I'm feeling that weight now and it's hard not to collapse under it.

I point to the right when we reach the end of the driveway, and Chris turns out onto the two lane county road. "Where are we going?" he wants to know.

"To a hunting cabin. One that Dad took Jake and me to several times. It's like over fifty years old, but will probably be there for another hundred. I'm not even sure who it belongs to, but there was never anyone else there when we went."

"Right. The cabin from the note. I thought maybe he meant the professor's place."

"No, I never met Mr. Hassan before Dad died. He didn't even live here then. So I figure he has to be talking about a place that only Jake or I would know, like with the duck blind. That letter wouldn't make sense to someone else reading it." We ride in silence for a while and I watch the line in the road rush at us.

Jake calls out my name and I turn to check on him. Baxter is draped over him in place of a blanket and he is curled up under his paws. He must have fallen right back to sleep, because he appears to be saying my name in a dream. Setting a hand gently on his forehead, I try to reassure him. Shuddering, he sighs and turns over, holding onto Baxter's leg like it's a teddy bear. I double-check the guns on the floor to make sure they are secured with safeties on and then turn back around.

"Do you think he could be right?" Looking back out at the trees creating a dark tunnel for us to travel through, I ask Chris my greatest fear.

"Right about what?"

"Not about wanting to change. There isn't anything that would excuse the murder of millions of people. I mean about God. Is it possible he did this? I mean, he sent plagues on the Egyptians before. Do you think this *is* God's plan?"

This time it's Chris's turn to smile without it reaching his eyes, but for him, it isn't due to a lack of emotion. Sadness is all I see as he stares back at me. "Absolutely not," he answers without hesitation. "Our God is a loving God; he wouldn't do this to us. Even during the times of Revelations, it is made clear that we will always have a *choice*.

"The Egyptians also had a choice. They were given numerous opportunities, actually. The greatest commandment is to love each other and to not murder. He wouldn't take away our ability to love or drive us to murder millions of people. That's the work of evil, Alex, not God."

I know that he's right, that even in the letters from my dad he refers twice now to this virus being *evil*. The professor has come to see the changes caused by the virus as a step forward in evolution and doesn't want to be left behind. To deal with his guilt he has to come up with an excuse to make it okay, and blaming it all on God is an easy out.

"We need to hurry." A new sense of urgency has overcome my fatigue and doubt. "We can't let this happen. It has to be stopped."

Reaching out across the seat, Chris takes hold of my hand. The physical contact reassures me that I'm not alone and I push aside all my fears. I need to concentrate on finding the cabin and moving forward.

"There's a gas station up here a ways, isn't there? We should stop and get some stuff. I'm starving."

I can't believe he's thinking about food. "We don't have time for that, Chris! People are probably dying *right now*! And what if they're looking for us? We can't risk being seen anywhere."

"Alex, think about it. How long until we're at the cabin? Then what? I guarantee you there is going to be some sort of traveling and hiking involved if we have to go find this lost pyramid. When was the last time that any of us ate or drank water? Do you even have any left with you? Because I don't. I think we're going to need some energy or else we'll fail. That isn't an option."

Looking at him, I weigh what he's saying. I hate how reasonable he can be, making me feel a little stupid and childish. Ultimately, I give in. "All right. But I only have a few bucks and we don't dare use a bank card."

"I've got almost twenty dollars. It should be enough for water and snacks. We'll park out of sight and you guys can stay in the truck. I've got sunglasses and a ball cap in my backpack and I won't say anything. I doubt their resources are that organized yet."

Half an hour later we're back on the road, eating a late dinner of cheese crackers and pepperoni sticks. Chris was right and the guy didn't seem to give him a second thought.

Jake woke up after we stopped for food and I've tried to explain what was going on, without being too elaborate. He seems to have accepted things for what they are and the rest has also helped. He's at least eating, and even laughed at Baxter trying to lick the peanut butter off his cracker.

We're deep in the Cascade Mountains now, heading northwest. We turned off the main road a ways back and the blacktop eventually gave way to gravel. Chris is forced to slow down to navigate the narrow, rutted road and I'm doing my best to watch for the markers that I vaguely remember.

As we come around one particularly steep bend,

Jacob calls out from the back seat. "Hey! There's that one sign with the moose head on it! I always thought that one was kinda cool."

Chris stops and I lean over him to peer through the driver's side window. Barely visible under outstretched cedar branches, is a brown marker with a moose head at the top, marking the trail.

"Good job, Jake!" I tell my brother. His help really has been critical. I take a moment to look at him closely, dreading a time when he might start to sniffle or show other signs of the flu invading his body. What I can see of him looks rather normal and I try to focus on the task at hand.

"Okay, Chris. I don't know if the truck will fit through there or not, but maybe we can manage to get it off this road." I jump out to help guide him in between the trees, pulling some branches aside to make room. It's a tight fit, but he's able to go a couple hundred feet up the barely recognizable road before having to come to a stop. There is a downed tree and it's way too big to even consider trying to move it. We'll be on foot from here.

Gathering all of our stuff, Chris takes the heavier bag with the skull, tucking the handgun into his pants. I sling the rifle across my back and his backpack with the food and ammo. I am especially thankful for the flashlight Chris brought. Once all the lights go out on the truck, the dim moonlight barely penetrates the thick canopy of trees and we are plunged into a complete darkness.

Jacob moves close to me, and I put an arm around him. He has never liked the dark. Before we set out,

Chris walks back to the head of the trail and takes a couple of minutes to bend the sign over. It's buried too deep for him to pull it out, but in a short time, he has it almost flat on the ground and I doubt anyone would notice it driving by. That isn't something I would have thought of and I'm thankful he's so smart.

"I don't have any shoes!" Jake complains. Looking down at his pajama-clad body, I see that he is indeed barefoot. I hadn't even thought about it.

Going back to the truck, I rummage around in the back seat for a while and come up with some running shoes I had stored in there from cross-country season. They are two sizes too big for him, but I tie them on as tight as possible and they seem to do the job.

"How far is it?" Chris asks me as we help each other climb over the large tree trunk. Giant mushrooms are growing all over the surface, making it slippery.

"I'm not sure, exactly," I admit. "We had always driven all the way to the cabin. Dad borrowed this cool jeep from one of the other cops he worked with, so we never had any problems getting there. I know it took several minutes so I'm guessing it's a good three miles or more."

"Well, at least we know no one else can make it up this road either," he observes. "And there aren't any other cars around. Odds are we're alone out here."

On the other side of the tree, I help Jacob down and Baxter easily leaps to the ground. My eyes have adjusted a bit to the dark and looking around at the woods surrounding us, I really hope that Chris is right.

TWENTY TWO

Saturday morning I wake up to a loud woodpecker banging on a nearby tree. Taking in my surroundings, I see a one-room cabin in the faint morning light and remember where we are. It was nearly two hours of walking through the dark mountains to get here last night. It must have been closer to five or six miles away and Chris had carried Jake on his back for most of it.

Chris is sprawled on the wooden floor, sound asleep. Baxter has decided he likes him, and is snuggled up close to keep warm. Jacob and I are sharing the one small cot in the space, with a thin blanket only big enough to cover our legs and half our bodies. When we had come camping here with Dad, we always brought foam pads and sleeping bags. Too bad none of that stuff was still here.

I never thought I would be able to sleep. Actually, at first, I had wanted to search for the clue and maybe set out again last night, but by the time we got here, it was obvious that wouldn't happen. Even though we were all beyond exhausted and emotionally drained, I figured my mind would keep racing or nightmares would plague me. I guess at some point though, the body just takes over, because I barely remember my head hitting the pillow and nothing else until now.

Having left our phones behind, I don't know what time it is, but I'm guessing still pretty early. Even so, I'm eager to get moving. With every passing minute, I'm afraid that more people are dying. I keep seeing that pit and imagine thousands of them all over the world. Shuddering, I pull the blanket up around my shoulders and close my eyes, trying to focus on the birds singing outside.

After a few minutes, my uncovered feet get too cold and I'm forced to acknowledge where I am and what is happening. Sitting up all the way, I re-adjust the blanket so that Jake is almost totally covered and carefully slide off the cot from behind him. Thankful that I had a sweatshirt with me yesterday, I pull the hood up to help hold in some body heat and slip into my shoes. Maybe that will help keep my feet warm.

My stomach grumbles and so I find the backpack with the food in it and decide on a breakfast of granola bar and yogurt covered raisins. After carefully counting how many bottles of water we have, I select one and only drink a third of it, since it will have to last me most of the day. Once again, I'm glad that Chris is with us and had insisted on stopping for the food. We would be in a lot of trouble if we didn't at least have the water. There is no water or electricity in this cabin and while there's a stream not too far away, it's never safe to drink it without boiling it first.

I pull the thin shade all the way up on the only window in the front of the cabin. It lets in enough light so that I can clearly see the huge stone fireplace that takes up the whole far wall. There's nothing fancy about this place, but it's obvious that whoever built it was a good craftsman and stone builder. It's probably local river rock that was hauled up here to build the hearth.

Moving closer to it, I start examining each rock, feeling along the crevasses that are filled with mortar. It reaches all the way to the ceiling and is ten feet wide. This might take a while.

"What are you doing?" I jump at the voice behind me and turn to find Chris propped up on one elbow watching me, petting a seemingly content Baxter.

"Do you remember what the note from my dad said about this cabin?"

"I have a good memory," he says, getting up. "But not *that* good. What did it say?" Baxter watches him with wishful eyes and then jumps up on the cot with Jacob when he realizes he isn't getting any more attention for now.

Going back to the bag, I take the letter out of the front pocket and hand it to him. I go back to my task as he reads that part to me. "Then you must go to the cabin and let its warmth guide you." "Oh … I get it. Those are a lot of rocks," he observes, looking up at the ceiling.

Getting a granola bar and water for himself, he joins me at the fireplace.

We search silently side-by-side for nearly an hour. My anxiety is steadily rising as it gets later and a sweat breaks out on my forehead. The stakes are way too high. This is taking too long. I'm thinking I should wake Jake and have him help us, when I go to put my hand on a small rock near the bottom back corner and pause. Getting down on all fours, I look closer at it to make sure. My heart quickens and I smile excitedly at Chris. "A vulture!" I exclaim, jumping up. "I think I found it!" Painted in black ink on the rock, low to the floor is a clear image of the hieroglyphic vulture.

Chris gets the flashlight and looks at it for himself, nodding in agreement. Pushing at the rock, he finds it solid. "I don't get it. Are we supposed to take it out or something, or does it mean that the fireplace is where we're supposed to look? Maybe it's on the *inside*. That *is* where it's warmest."

I take the flashlight from him and look again, contemplating what he's said. He could be right, but my instinct tells me otherwise. I am learning lately to follow my instinct. Running my fingers around the edge, I notice that while there is mortar, it's a lighter color than the rest. Perhaps because it isn't as old?

I look around the almost bare room, and settle on the fireplace set. Grabbing the wicked-looking poker, I use the pointed end to start chipping away at the cement around the rock. It's actually pretty soft and starts crumbling with just a few strikes from the metal.

"Smart," Chris says and I smile at his compliment. Jacob wakes up from the noise but sits silently on the cot watching me, absently petting his dog. His eyes look a bit glassy and red around the rims but I tell myself it's because of everything he's been through. Nothing else.

In less than ten minutes, I've scraped out enough that the rock is starting to wiggle and in another five, I hand the poker over to Chris and start working it with my hands.

When it finally comes free, I give a shout of triumph and look expectantly at the space behind it. My hopes falling, I shine the flashlight into it, sure that there must be something there. It's empty.

"Look at the rock, Alex." Not realizing Jake had come to stand beside me, I nearly drop the rock on my foot and then laugh at myself. Following his directions, I hold the freed rock up and sure enough, there is something written on the back of it in the same dark ink: 48°28'46.28N, 119°53'.46W

"They're just numbers!" Jacob complains, obviously disappointed.

"No. Not just numbers. They're GPS coordinates. Chris, do you have something you can write these down on?"

Digging back through the backpacks, he finally finds a small notebook and a broken pencil. I read the numbers off to him and then look once more at the rock to make sure there isn't anything else on it. Before setting it back in place, I scrape it across another rock until the ink is rubbed away. I sweep the mortar crumbs and dust into the cracks around the hearth so that it isn't obvious, remembering my dad's words that this information is sacred.

"That's got to be the location of the pyramid," I say, feeling a huge sense of relief as I stand and wipe the dust from my hands. Chris, however, doesn't seem to share my enthusiasm. He has a frown on his face and is looking rather frustrated.

"Well it's great and all, but unfortunately we have absolutely no way of locating those coordinates on a map," he states. "Remember, we don't have our phones. We'll have to go back to town and get one."

"No. I don't think we will." He just stares at me, and rather than try to explain, I walk over to the only cabinet in the room. Opening the bottom cupboard, I'm relieved to find the bag is still there. Dad always left this at the cabin, so we would have some essential items no matter what. Pulling out the medium sized, camouflaged duffle, I unzip it and start taking stuff out.

A decent first aid kit, emergency candle, stale energy bars, flint, a knife and finally at the bottom ... an old GPS unit. Holding it up so Chris can see it, I tell him why it was there. "Dad always liked to locate his favorite hunting spots and fishing holes with this. The mountains and woods around here are dense and steep so it would be easy to get lost. It's pretty ancient, but it works."

"Well thank goodness your dad was prepared!" His mood dramatically improved, Chris looks over the older device and tries the power button. To our relief, it turns on. Handing it back to me, I try to remember the right buttons to push and after a few minutes have it to where I can enter the new numbers. After searching for a satellite, the image finally comes up and it takes us awhile to make sense of the map.

"Oh man," Chris groans, after the reality of our situation sinks in. "That's got to be around 15 miles away from here in the middle of rugged terrain. Without knowing how to get there, we could spend *weeks* looking for it!" Running his hands through his thick hair, he paces the small room, unable to deal with the thought that we won't be able to stop this in time to save millions of lives.

As I look again at the map on the black and white screen, hoping to get some sort of inspiration, it goes dark. Pushing at the power button, it won't turn back on. "Great! Now the batteries are dead." Rummaging through what's left in the duffle bag, I check the front zippered pocket and thankfully find a pack of AA batteries. Slipping the back cover off the GPS unit, I feel my spirits rise.

"I think Dad took that all into consideration," I tell Chris as I pull out a small piece of folded up paper. I eagerly open it and read it out loud:

*"Alexis, you are almost there! Remember that incredible fishing hole we found the last time we came up here? There was that well marked deer **trail** across the water that we were going to go explore the next chance we got. Maybe you can do it for me. Love to you, Jacob and your mother."*

I hand the note over to Chris, put in the new batteries, and start playing with the GPS again. "Got it!"

I exclaim after a bit of searching. "Dad would save the locations, and the fishing hole was the last one on here. It's a mile away, and pretty easy to get to. I think the deer trail is going to lead us where we need to go, Chris. I'm sure he's marked it along the way. He came up here for a few days by himself the month before their trip to Egypt. This must have been why. We should be able to find it!"

Both of us smiling now, we again have a purpose and a plan. We get all of our stuff together, dividing it up between the two backpacks. I'm happy to add the flint, knife, and first aid kit. Looking over at Jake who has gone back to the cot, my smile fades. He doesn't look well. My stomach tightens with dread and I go over to him.

"Are you okay? Would you like a granola bar or something? You need to eat; we have a really big hike ahead of us."

Shaking his head, he refuses the food but accepts the water I offer. "My throat hurts, Alex. A lot. And why did Dad write all those notes to *you* and none to me?"

My worst fears confirmed, I put an arm around him and try not to let him see how upset I am. Chris is watching us closely, back to snuggling with Baxter. I notice that he's feeding the dog part of his granola bar, as I try to carefully choose my words.

"He only wrote me two other letters Jake, and they were more like riddles. I think it was only because I'm the oldest, and he thought I would have the best chance of figuring this stuff out. You know what, though? If it hadn't been for you, I would probably still be trying to find the *last* hiding place!"

He considers this carefully, and then smiles slightly. "Yeah, I guess you're right. I wish he were here though, he would know how to make Mom better."

"Well, we're lucky he was so smart, because he's told *us* how to find some special medicine that will make *everyone* better. I know you understand how important that is Jake and that even though you don't feel good, we have to leave."

"I guess that wasn't medicine Mom gave me last night," he says, wiping at his runny nose. "Do you think this other medicine Dad hid will make *me* better too?"

My heart breaking, I can't keep it together. Pulling him to me, I hold him tight so he can't see my face, silent tears falling on his head. A warm hand on my shoulder both consoles me and also reminds me that we don't have time. Not even for this.

Pulling away, I wipe roughly at my face with the sleeve of my sweatshirt and stand up. "Of course it's going to make you better, Jake! So we better hurry and go find it." Seemingly satisfied with my answer, he jumps from the cot and ties on my over-sized shoes.

As we step out into the daylight, I look up through the trees and see that the sun is almost directly overhead. Almost half the day is gone and I can feel the time rapidly slipping away. With GPS in hand, I lead us out across a small meadow behind the cabin and towards the towering mountains of the Cascades.

TWENTY THREE

The day is warming up fast, and within a few minutes, I have my sweatshirt off and tied around my waist. The sky is clear and shining like a bright gem over us, contrasting with the dark thoughts that fill my head.

We're trying to set a fast pace, but between the terrain and Jacob's feet it's taking longer than I would like. Everything looks different from what I remember so it's a good thing we have the GPS or I probably wouldn't even be able to find the fishing spot. Reaching the edge of the meadow, we scramble up a steep incline into the trees and then walk along the crest. The plan is that once we're even with the location on the map, we can then hopefully cut across to it.

Jacob and Baxter have wandered ahead a ways, so I take the opportunity to talk quietly with Chris about something that's been bothering me. "I don't understand why they would choose a skull as a piece in all of this.

Isn't that normally a symbol of death? I swear that all the other secret societies and cults out there have some sort of pyramid shape, eye, or skull in its literature. It just seems out of place."

"Actually, the idea of a skull representing death is relatively new, historically speaking," he explains, surprising me that he would even know something about it. "In ancient times, it was a symbol of life or re-birth. I suspected that it would need to be placed inside a pyramid as soon as I saw it, because of Native American legend."

"Seriously?"

"Yup. There are a whole bunch of various legends in different cultures about the skulls. That's part of the mystery. The one I'm familiar with states that there are thirteen skulls that speak or sing. It says that there will be a time of great need and crisis for humanity. The crystal skulls will be brought together to reveal their knowledge. This is vital to the survival of the human race. Kinda hard to write all of that off as a coincidence, don't you think?"

"I guess that when I did my research on them, I missed that part," I say, amazed at how so many things were connected.

"According to a Cherokee medicine man, the skulls are supposed to be put in a pyramid, and when they are all arranged in a certain order, they will communicate with the corresponding planets. That, along with all the other beliefs surrounding them, makes me think that there is a mix of part truths in each culture. I think that when the pyramid was built up here, and the Khufu Bast was watching it, the Native American myths and stories grew around that."

"Communicate with the planets," I repeat, lost in thought. "How farfetched do you think that is now? We already know this virus is alien since it came here on a meteor. We have no idea how a civilization thousands of years ago could have had such advanced technology to create an anti-virus and these skulls. There are all sorts of theories that Egyptians have alien origins or had alien visitors. Man ... this gives me the creeps."

"I don't know Alex; at this point I'm willing to say that anything is possible. One of the reasons all those other groups you're talking about incorporate pyramids into their symbolism is due to all the mystery surrounding the Egyptians. You know, it's one of the first major cities discussed in the Bible and some great men of God came from Egypt, including Moses."

This makes me stop, and he looks back at me questioningly. "I guess I didn't know that," I say, thinking about all the implications behind it. I wish I had read my Bible now or at least paid more attention in Sunday school. I know through other conspiracy theories that regardless of your faith, it's a pretty accurate historical document.

Not sure whether I'm glad to have started this conversation or not, I hurry to catch up with Jake, not wanting to let him out of my sight. He is being very brave and not complaining, but I can tell he is getting worse. He took his pajama top off and tied it around himself, like I did my sweatshirt, but he is holding one of the sleeves in his hand to use for his nose. It's a regular faucet, and he's developing bags under his eyes. I talked him into eating a candy bar, but that's all he's had since last night. I'm afraid it's all going to catch up with him soon and he won't be able to go very far before having to be carried.

Ticking away, ticking away. I look up again at the sun, and am dismayed to see that it's starting its march down the other side of the sky. How can it already be past noon? Holding the GPS out in front of me, I scrutinize it for a minute. We have to be getting close. A little blinking arrow indicates our approximate location and we are in fact coming up parallel with our destination.

"Jake! Start going down the hill to your right," I call out.

We all carefully make our way to the bottom, and two-hundred feet further west, we encounter a stream running south. Finally, I recognize something.

"That little waterfall! I know where we are!" Following the water downstream, I scoot past the waterfall flowing over moss-covered rocks and around a small bend. Just as I hoped, this opens up to a small cove where the water backs up against large boulders before spilling past them.

A deep pool is created, and on the far side, there is an area of trampled grass where deer obviously come on a daily basis. "There! That's the trail!" I say excitedly, looking for the best way across the water.

We all walk back to the bend where it's only ten feet

wide and a foot or two deep. Taking off our shoes and rolling up our pants, we wade across. The water is from high up in the mountains and ice cold, so I'm thankful we don't have to go for a real swim.

Baxter is overcome with excitement. He loves the water and immediately begins running up and down the stream, snapping at imaginary fish and jumping around. It takes us a few minutes to rein him in but eventually he figures out we are leaving and follows us.

Once we reach the spot where the grass is all trampled, he goes crazy again, this time running around with his nose to the ground, barking loudly. Apparently finding some fresh deer turds, he happily rolls in it like any good dog would do.

While running away from my poop-covered dog, I stumble over a small boulder strategically placed in the middle of the trail about twenty feet back from the water. Fighting off his apologetic kisses, I look a little closer at it and then smile, not minding the smell so much.

Painted again in black ink on the rock is the vulture. "Chris, Jacob!" I call out, standing up and brushing myself off. "Look, Dad is leaving us markers. This is the way to go!"

Relieved to have confirmation that we are going the right way, I clear out the GPS and enter the new coordinates for what will hopefully lead us to the pyramid. As it comes up, it's clear that we are getting closer and are headed in the right general direction.

"I think that we definitely should follow this deer trail, but watch carefully for anything that might indicate another path," I suggest, hoping Chris will agree with me.

"Makes sense," he says, taking up the lead. "I'll bet he stays consistent. We should keep an eye out for rocks that look out of place."

Jacob follows him and I go last since there isn't enough room for anything other than single file. Looking back to make sure that Baxter is with us, for a moment I think I see movement from the other side of the fishing hole. Freezing, I hold my breath and watch. After a minute, I slowly breathe out and relax a little. It must have been my imagination. Turning, I jog to catch up, Baxter at my heels.

As I reach Jacob, I realize what it was that seemed so off. While I was staring across the water, there wasn't any other sound. No birds, no frogs ... nothing. Glancing behind me again, the back of my neck tingling, I get the intense feeling that we are being watched.

TWENTY FOUR

We've been walking for hours and night is closing in on us. I shared my concerns with Chris as soon as I could without alarming Jake, but we haven't seen anything else and Baxter seems calm. Of course, with all the other animals out here and the new, exciting smells, it wouldn't surprise me if he were thrown off a bit.

It's not as if we have other options, anyway. Our only choice right now is to keep going as fast as possible. Jake is deteriorating rapidly. Chris has been carrying him on his back for the last couple of hours and it's taking its toll. The ground is uneven, steep in places and with logs or rocks to climb over in what seems an endless landscape.

The last time I put my hand to his forehead, he was burning up, and the glands in his neck are visibly swelling. He is draped loosely over Chris right now and I'm afraid he won't even be able to hang on to his shoulders for much longer and will have to be carried in his arms. This will slow us down even further and the only thing driving me through this madness right now is the belief that we are about to find this blasted pyramid and wake up from our nightmare.

We find three other markers along the way, leading us off on other smaller, even less defined paths. We've made decent progress in spite of the odds and my best guess is that we're within a mile or so of our destination. Problem is it's been a good hour since we saw any sign that we were even still on a trail, and I'm afraid we might be going the wrong way now. It's getting hard to see the image on the GPS, so I've taken to shining the flashlight on it. I'm trying not to do it too much to conserve the batteries. It's the only one we have.

Stopping, I try to get my bearings. I've been leading us for a while now, and hold up my hand to indicate to Chris what I'm doing. "What do you think?" he asks tiredly, shifting Jake's weight from one side to the other.

"We're close," I assure him, looking around on the ground with the flashlight. "I don't see any sign of that path anymore, Chris. Maybe it doesn't matter now, so long as there aren't any ravines or big hills between here and there. Should we just try to keep going to it in a straight line?"

"What else can we do?" He says logically.

"I'm thirsty," Jake moans, sliding down from Chris's back. As his feet hit the ground, he stumbles and almost falls. Chris catches his arms and helps steady him.

"Here," I say, handing him the last bottle of water.

As he takes it from my hand, Baxter begins to growl a warning. Startled, I direct the flashlight towards the trees he's pointing at and gasp when a set of eyes a good six feet off the ground glow back. "Shiners!" I yell, panic washing over me.

Chris moves so fast that I hardly register him scooping Jake up before he's running past me, and I force myself into motion. Shadows come to life as I follow them and dodge low hanging branches, weaving through the towering trees. Darkness chases and then surrounds us, making it harder to see. Resisting the urge to look behind me, I expect to be grabbed at any second. This causes my adrenaline to surge through me and propels my legs even faster.

Finally, I catch up to Chris, who is struggling to hold onto a terrified Jacob. He's squirming, trying to get free and Chris is telling him to keep still. I'm about to call out to them when the tree trunk near my head suddenly explodes, sending out splinters, some of which find my face.

Falling to the ground, I instinctively cover my head with my arms and roll away, waiting for the next bullet to find my back. When the impact doesn't happen, I remember that I have a rifle slung over my shoulder and scramble onto my stomach. Propped on my elbows, I slide the backpack off first, and then bring the rifle around and up to my shoulder, chambering a round in the same motion. Struggling to see in the dim light, I try to distinguish the trees from other shadows and look for anything moving.

"Alex!" Chris whispers, much closer than I would have guessed. Looking behind and to my left, I can just make out him and Jacob on the ground.

"I'm okay!" I croak, looking quickly back in the other direction, sure someone is sneaking up on us. I wipe at something in my right eye and realize that it's blood. Feeling my forehead, I find several cuts from the flying wood, but nothing serious. Nothing I can do about it right now.

How did they find us? How could they have followed us or even known where we were going? Maybe Professor Hassan decided to get in on the movement early, or even more likely, the guy at the gas station called someone. I have a feeling things are more connected and organized than we could have ever guessed. If Mom really is a genius, then it wouldn't have been hard for her to figure out that I wasn't actually sick and was up to something. Especially if she saw that book. That would explain why I was allowed to go on for so long; they were just waiting for me to make this move. Feeling stupid, I scan the area in front of me with a great desire to shoot something. I hope my mom isn't out there though, because this time I won't be able to hesitate.

Baxter must be guarding Jake, because he starts growling again from behind me and Chris tries to silence him. It doesn't work though and the growling gets louder and turns into a high-pitch bark that I have never heard him make. My skin crawls as the fight-or-flight instinct in me battles it out. Finger on the trigger, I frantically search for whatever it is that Baxter sees.

Sensing movement to my right, I start to bring my rifle around, but before I can, a shot rings out, immediately answered by my dad's 45 that Chris has. He must have missed, because the Shiner steps out from behind a tree to get a better shot, but I'm ready. Taking aim for the dimly luminescent eyes, I pull the trigger and am assured by the following thud of a body hitting the ground.

Holding the rifle in my right hand, I hook my left arm through the backpack straps and pick up the flashlight. Crawling on my stomach, I make my way over to Chris, who's moaning. Jake is saying his name and crying, and I refuse to acknowledge what it all means.

I quickly reach them and assess what's happened. Chris is on his back, holding his side where blood is rapidly flowing out between his fingers. I put my left hand over his and look into his eyes. "You can't leave me," I say hoarsely, fighting back the tears. "We aren't done yet."

Smiling slightly, he puts one of his bloodied hands on top of mine. "I don't plan on going anywhere, Tiger Eyes, but you have to keep moving. I have faith in you, Alex. It's what you are meant to do."

Encouraged by his words, I look around us, fearful that there are other Shiners and not knowing what to do next. Closing my eyes, I take a slow cleansing breath and try to listen to my instincts. An owl hoots in the distance, calling to me, and a slight breeze blows through my hair. The night then becomes very still and I am aware of a growing pressure, like the weight that I have been bearing is about to come crashing down. Chris is right. As hard as this is, there are bigger things happening and I have to move. Now.

Untying my sweatshirt, I wad it up and put it under his t-shirt, over his wound. "Jacob," I say, turning to him. His skin glows white in the pale moonlight that is starting to show through the trees. Eyes wide and glassy with fever, he looks at me with desperation. "I need you to push down on this like I am. Keep pressure on it. Can you do that?"

Nodding his head, he places his hands where I show him and sits down next to Chris. I hug him tight, refusing to let myself think it's for the last time, and then check the 45 to make sure it is ready to shoot and place it in Chris's bloody hands. "There might be more Shiners. In fact, it wouldn't make sense if there wasn't. Can you do it?"

"I'll be okay for a while, I think." he says softly, as I prop him up against a tree. Rummaging through our bags, I come up with the emergency candle, first aid kit, and flint. I place it all next to him, and then take the bag with the skull, and rifle ammo.

With Chris and Baxter watching the trees, I risk clicking on the flashlight to look at the GPS. Amazingly, we ran in the right direction and are even closer to it now. Walking over to the fallen Shiner, I confirm that I hit my mark. It isn't Mom. Going back, I shut the light off and reach for my rifle leaning next to Chris.

Before I can pick it up, Baxter rushes past me snarling and leaps just as Mr. Jones comes into view, gun raised in my direction. Latching onto his arm, Baxter forces him to drop the gun and then won't let go. I try and aim my rifle, but can't get a clear shot. Jacob starts screaming his dog's name, and I watch in terror as the man that used to be our friend takes hold of Baxter's neck with his free hand. His intent is clear and there is no way I'm letting it happen.

Rushing forward, I raise my rifle like a club and hit Mr. Jones across the head as hard as I can. With a sickening thud, he falls to his knees but doesn't go down. Baxter releases his arm but is obviously dazed and making an odd wheezing noise.

I take a couple of steps back and try to finish him, but he's already moving with incredible speed in the opposite direction. I take a parting shot, but it slams harmlessly into a tree he just ran past.

Reassured somewhat by the gun he left behind, I pick it up and hand it off to Chris. "Maybe he's the last one," I suggest. "I think they would have come at us at the same time, otherwise."

Baxter has recovered, and is growling again. Going to him, I place a hand on his loyal head and call him a good dog. He's not having any of it though, and his agitation grows. I take hold of his collar and try to tell him to stay. I can't lose him now, not after all of this. But it's like he's gone wild, and he starts twisting and pulling away from me. "Baxter! Stop it! It's okay. Stay!" The worn leather collar he arrived with nearly two years ago can't keep him back any longer. It snaps in half and I am left holding it in my hand as Baxter heads for the trees.

"Baxter!" all three of us yell at the same time. I glance down at the broken collar before tossing it and pause. Picking up the flashlight I had dropped, I look closely at the leather and then back at where Baxter disappeared. Burned into its underside is yet another image of the vulture.

"I have to follow him!" I tell Chris, and toss the strap at him as I run off after my dog, my loyal friend that was always meant to see me through this to the end.

TWENTY FIVE

Crashing through the woods with my rifle at the ready, I'm trying my best to keep sight of Baxter up ahead of me. Every once in a while he'll pause and look back at me to make sure I'm still there, but he isn't wasting any time.

I try not to think too much. We are beyond things making sense and so I just follow my dog with the confidence that he will take me to the pyramid. Knowing that Chris and Jacob are left somewhere in the mountains behind me, spurs me on and gives me more energy than should be possible.

After ten or fifteen minutes, I jump over a fallen cedar tree and almost trip over Baxter who is sitting on the other side. Tongue hanging, eyes bright, he looks at me expectantly. "What?" I ask him.

He barks at me once in response, shuffles to his right a few feet, and then barks again. Feeling exposed, I remove the backpack and take out the GPS. Hating to turn the flashlight on, I look to see where we are and find that we are right on top of the coordinates. Feeling both excited and frustrated, I turn the light away from me and start looking around.

Mostly surrounded by trees, I don't know where I'm supposed to go. I guess I expected to just walk into a clearing with a pyramid in the middle of it, but there is neither a clearing nor a pyramid. Stepping closer to Baxter, I notice that the steep hillside behind him is more than just earth.

Dropping to my knees, I dig at the dirt with my hands. The soft, loamy soil comes up easily and ten inches down, I encounter smooth, flat rock. Standing up again, I try to grasp what I am looking at. It isn't a hill. Well, I mean it looks like one, but I don't think it is. If the pyramid has been here for thousands of years than it could very well be reclaimed by the forest.

Walking up the steep incline twenty feet, I again dig at the surface and this time it's only six inches down to the same chiseled stone. There are trees here, but they are thin and the roots are exposed, like you would expect to see on the rocky edge of a cliff or something. I believe I am standing on top of the pyramid.

My heart racing, I run back down to the bottom and start following the slope, looking for anything that might indicate an opening. "Come on, Baxter! Find the door!" I call to him, hoping that he understands.

After a hundred feet, I encounter large rocks jutting out, covered in moss. Running my hands over them, I notice that although the corners are worn and rounded, it's clear that these used to be symmetrical blocks of stone, spaced about ten feet apart. Tearing at the branches, roots, and vines growing and hanging down in between them, I know that I'm standing at the entrance.

Once I have made an opening large enough to fit through, I turn the flashlight back on and call to Baxter.

"*Alexis ...*"

Jumping back, I aim the light into the darkness beyond, where my whispered name came from. I can't see anything, and so step through towards my destiny.

The passageway is long and narrow, reminding me of the tunnel in my dreams. Looking carefully at the rock walls on either side of me, I am not surprised to see hieroglyphics. After a couple of bends to the right and then the left, it opens up into a large central chamber, the ceiling too high above me for the weak light to reach. The fluttering of wings assures me that I am not alone.

My breath coming now in quick, ragged gasps, I move to the center of the room. To my dismay, there isn't any obvious sign of where I'm supposed to place the skull. Slipping the straps off my shoulders, I'm thankful to set it down and carefully remove the crystal skull. Not sure what I should do next, I put it on the dirt floor.

Baxter comes to me, sniffing. He looks at the skull and then me, trying to figure out whether he should be concerned or not. Chuffing, he moves past me and starts walking in a circle, nose to the floor. His excitement growing, he begins to dig and I silently watch him.

As some sort of rock formation comes into view, I

get in on the action and start to claw at the dirt alongside him. Before long, we've uncovered a platform about 1x1 foot. My first thought is that I should place the skull in the middle, but when I run my hand over it to wipe off more of the dirt, I realize there is a small depression in the center. Getting down close to it, I blow some dirt out of the small crevasses and then use the flashlight to inspect it.

It is indeed an impression, and if I'm right, it's the reverse of the image on my wooden medallion. Our family crest. My hands shaking, I pull it out from under my shirt and slip the chain over my head. As I suspected, it's a perfect fit, and as it slides into place, there is a deep, booming click from far under me and the ground shudders. I cry out in alarm when the whole floor starts to drop away from the walls, and I find myself descending below the surface like an ancient elevator.

After ten feet, I see new walls take shape and torches spaced around the newly formed room flash to life. I'm guessing the fresh oxygen created some sort of chemical reaction. Five more feet and it groans to a stop and I can clearly see another entrance on the far side of the huge, underground room.

Afraid to remove the medallion in case it might make us rise back up, I leave it there and pick up the skull. There are more torches leading down another hallway on the other side of the opening, so I head that way.

With Baxter walking softly beside me, we follow the light and go another couple hundred feet before reaching yet *another* room. This one is even larger than the first, but brightly illuminated with what must be a dozen torches. Looking more closely at them, I see that it isn't even fire, but some sort of gas burning. Or at least, that is the closest comparison my brain can come up with. I remind myself that this was built with technology greater than what we have today, and don't waste any time trying to figure it out.

In the center is what appears to be a huge spiral staircase, also illuminated. Crossing to it, I look up into its depths and feel a strong sense of peace wash over me. I start to climb.

It seems like forever that I am ascending the stairs, and I wonder how something made of stone could be so tall yet not fall over. Just when I think that I can't make it another step, I break through into a room and I'm disoriented for a moment. The floor is covered in what were once rich, woven mats, the walls angling to a point fifty feet above me in what has to be the top of the pyramid. The stone is decorated with familiar, ancient hieroglyphs mixed in with double helix DNA strands and other odd shapes that I've never seen before.

Set in one of the three walls, across from the stairwell, is a recessed space two feet square and three feet off the floor, filled with light. I am drawn to it, and my breath catches in my throat when I see a hollowed nook in the floor of it that I am betting to be a perfect match with the skull.

Relieved to be rid of its weight, both literal and implied, I gingerly set the crystal in place. It fits like I knew it would. Leaning my rifle and flashlight against the wall, I step back to look at it and notice a finely carved wooden crucifix attached to the wall just above the opening. I know that it had to have been put there by either the last sentinel during the 1700's or else my dad, since this pyramid was built before Christ was even born and Christianity wasn't known here until then. Seeing it helps solidify in my mind that God's plan has always been to set us free, and that it is my father's final marker. I made it.

With renewed hope, I look at the blood on my right hand ... my blood, and face the skull. Closing my eyes, I send a prayer for success, then reach out, and smear it across the pyramid on the skull's forehead.

TWENTY SIX

Nothing happens. Crouched down, I am at eye level with the skull, staring into its empty sockets. I expected it to at least light up or something, but there is no indication that anything changed. "No, no, no," I mutter, backing away from it. This can't end like this. It *has* to work! Clawing desperately at the clotting wounds on my forehead, I manage to get a fresh supply of blood oozing down my face and run my fingers through it. Maybe it was just too dry.

Stepping back up to the skull, I wipe the wet blood over the pyramid carving. Then, for good measure, I smear it around the whole thing, in case it's supposed to go somewhere else. Now it looks like it's wearing some macabre war paint and has a sinister appearance. Shaking my head at its lack of activity, I don't know what else to do. I wish that Chris were here. He would have an idea. He's the smart one.

"Having problems, dear?"

I spin around at the raspy voice behind me and

discover that Mr. Jones is emerging from the stairwell. Baxter's hair rises on his back, and he growls menacingly. That Baxter didn't even hear him coming proves how stealthy the Shiners are. I can't help but notice the large hunting knife in his left hand, the odd light from the torches glinting off the metal.

"Why are you doing this?" I ask, looking around the room for anything I can use as a weapon. I chastise myself for setting the rifle down. It's too far away. By the time I could reach it, he'd be on me. Other than the mats, the floor is bare. He begins walking slowly, tauntingly towards me with that odd grin on his face. Baxter must sense that he is at a disadvantage and stays by my side instead of attacking.

"Because this is what the world needs. A time of renewal and union. Once we are ready, *they* will come back, and we can't let you **stop it**." He shouts the last words, his eyes glowing brighter, the grin turning to a sneer.

I back up to the wall, with the skull behind me and the cross pressing into my neck. I raise my hands above my head in a pleading gesture. "Please, don't hurt me," I beg.

"Oh I'm not going to *hurt* you," he assures me, moving to within a couple of feet. "I'm going to *kill* you!"

He closes the last of the space between us and I grab desperately at the cross on the wall behind me, bringing it around. As he raises the knife to plunge down into my chest, I surprise him by stepping forward to meet him.

Lunging with all my strength, I come up under his arms, ramming the tip of the cross into his stomach and we fall back onto the floor together.

Appalled at what I've had to do, I roll away from him. He's dropped the knife and is looking down in astonishment at the carving that is protruding from his mid-section. "I'm so sorry," I whisper, scooting back on all fours.

Blood is rapidly pooling beneath him and his head falls back as his breathing slows, becoming ragged. I gag at the coppery stench of his blood and sit back on my heels, not knowing what to do. Eyes fluttering, he gasps once, and then focuses on my nearby form.

"Alexis," he whispers, reaching out to me with great effort. Looking into his eyes, I see the kind Mr. Jones I've known all my life. Loud, violent sobs rack my body as I lean forward and take hold of his offered hand. Baxter stops barking and lies beside us, whimpering. "It's okay, dear," he says softly. "Thank you." Closing his eyes, his hand goes limp and I know that he is gone.

Burying my head in my arms, I cry for Mr. Jones and everyone else that I am unable to help. This was all for nothing. My blood isn't pure enough. Now I have lost all the people that I love and there is nothing left for me. Baxter licks my face, and I wrap my arms around his neck. "I still have you, don't I buddy?" Although he is a big dog, he somehow manages to climb into my lap.

We stay that way for several minutes, consoling each other. I finally get enough of a grip to contemplate how I can drag Chris back to the cabin, if he's still alive.

Looking down at my hands resting in Baxter's fur, I see that they are covered in blood and can't help but feel like it represents the blood of the world.

I know that in reality the blood on my right hand is mostly mine. Mr. Jones's blood is still damp on my left forearm, and the rest of it that covers my left hand is all Chris's. So much blood, swimming with both infected and uninfected DNA. I wonder briefly if I've now been exposed, or if Chris's purest DNA would somehow offset the effect. Wait.

Sitting up with a jolt, I startle Baxter and he leaps off my lap. "My blood isn't good enough Baxter, because I'm only fifty percent Egyptian," I explain to my friend, who stares at me with interest. "But Chris is seventy-five percent Okanogan Indian, a tribe that is native to this region. Native Americans have been in this area for thousands of years, back when this pyramid was built."

Excited now, I get to my feet and go back to the crystal skull, my smeared blood dried on its surface. With cautious hope, I place my left hand on the forehead of the skull and push against it. Almost immediately, it starts to vibrate. Crying with relieved joy, I step back from it and watch as it begins to glow, intricate patterns of light running throughout the inside of it.

As the intensity builds, the vibration spreads to first the walls and then the floor. A low hum fills the air and the hairs on my arms stand on end. Kneeling down on the floor, I hold onto Baxter as light gathers in the space over our heads.

With a low rumbling sound and the scraping of rock

against rock, the top fifty feet of the pyramid lifts off above us and rises up into the night sky, dirt, and small trees rolling down it. After everything that has happened, I'm still not prepared for such a site, and I'm mesmerized by it.

Energy pulsates in the air around me and reaches a crescendo as it starts to crackle. Tendrils of electricity reach out from the piece hovering, and it begins to spin. Slowly at first, but then it quickly gains momentum. Faster and faster it goes, until huge bolts of light shoot out from multiple directions, reaching out through the night sky to places unseen.

"The anti-virus," I say with certainty. "We've done it!" I think back to what the professor had said and now Mr. Jones and I know that this might be only the beginning. But what the creators of the virus don't understand is the human desire to fight for our freedom and our value of life. To simply be alive isn't enough.

A thicker beam of light erupts from the top of the spinning triangle and then out the bottom, engulfing me. As I gaze up into what I hope is our cure, letting it wash over me, I finally realize that our greatest gift, and weapon, is love. I mean, who can ever win against something as powerful as that?

With a renewed sense of purpose, I gather my stuff and then turn and head for the stairwell. Pausing at Mr. Jones's body, I only wish that he had been a few minutes later. I take some peace in knowing that he is with his wife. I have no doubt now that there is so much more to this life than what we can simply see. My dad will always be with me, and will be waiting for me when it's my time to move on. But that won't be tonight.

The light continues to intensify behind me while I begin my descent. It takes much less time going down the stairs than it did to come up. When I reach the platform with my medallion still in place, I pull it out and like I suspected, the room starts to slowly scrape back up into its original position. I put the chain back over my head and turn on my flashlight as Baxter and I rise up into the dark chamber.

Half expecting to be greeted by a group of Shiners, I am relieved to find that I'm alone. Making my way back through the long tunnels, I creep quietly to the opening of the pyramid. Baxter walks out first, sniffing at the ground but otherwise at ease. I follow him closely, looking out into the woods for any sign of someone waiting for us. It's hard to believe that only a few of them would have come for me. Not after what Mr. Jones said. Even if the anti-virus works, there's no way to know how long it will take for them to be cured. That's assuming they'll ever really *be* normal again.

With each passing minute that I'm not attacked, my confidence grows and eventually I'm running, frantic to get back to Jake and Chris. The emotions from the past days are beginning to catch up to me and tears begin blurring my vision as I hurtle through the trees.

When I can't find them after half an hour, I panic and start calling out, not caring anymore who hears me. Sitting on the cooling ground, all I hear in return is the hooting of an owl. I turn to my friend. "Baxter, find

Jake!" Baxter gives me one of his classic looks and seems to understand. Barking excitedly, he tears off to my right and then through some bushes in the distance. I quickly follow, not noticing the scratches on my arms as I push through the branches after him. I'm just in time to see him running up a slope and his bark has changed pitch.

"Baxter! Alex! Is that you?" I can barely hear it, but begin to cry even harder at the sound of Chris's voice. He's alive! Scurrying up the hill after my dog, I try to answer him, but only a sob comes out.

Once at the top, I can see them in the distance. They've lit the emergency candle, and Baxter is jumping around Jacob, who is not only standing on his own, but also hoping up and down. And he's smiling. My flashlight gives me away and Jake comes running to me. I drop down on my knees and gather him up in a fierce hug. His face is cool, the fever gone. Could it really happen that fast?

"You did it, Alex! I knew you would! Is that what the light is? I'm already starting to feel better. What happened? What did you do?"

Pulling away from me, he searches my face for answers. "It's hard to explain," I whisper, my voice weak with emotion. "But Dad showed me. He always looked out for us, Jake. He still loves you, don't ever forget that."

Taking his face in my hands, I look closely at him. He actually does look almost normal. There are still bags under his eyes, but his color is good. "When did you start feeling better?" I quiz him, still afraid to believe it.

229

"I dunno. I guess a little bit after that light thingy. My throat doesn't even hurt anymore! Do we have any food? I'm hungry." Smiling, I hug him again. Now he really sounds like himself.

Taking my hand, he starts to pull me towards Chris. "We need to take him to the doctor," he tells me. "Do you think it's safe?"

Following him in a daze, I try to focus on his questions. "I'm not sure. We'll get him back to the cabin though, and then we'll figure out what to do." I allow him to lead me into the candlelight.

"Told ya I wasn't going anywhere." Still propped against the tree, Chris looks pale, but seems alert. I'm fighting the familiar urge to hug him, but decide to give in to it. Kneeling down beside him, I do my best to wrap my arms around his shoulders without hurting him. He returns the embrace, holding me close. The rest of my fear melts away and for the first time since this nightmare started, I almost feel safe.

Pointing up at the rays of light spreading out across the night, he grins. "I'm assuming you have something to do with that?"

Turning to sit down beside him, I look up at the display. "Well, kinda. But to be honest, it couldn't have happened without *you*. Or your blood." Judging by the odd look that he's giving me, it's obvious he wants some answers. "There *is* a pyramid. I— I don't even know how to describe it. What happened inside, I mean. I'll explain it later once we're out of here. I just can't … do it right now." To my relief, he doesn't push it.

"What about the Khufu Bast and the Mudameere? If what the professor said is right, then this might only be the first part of their plan, even if the anti-virus works on everyone."

Fighting the new fear that threatens to take over, I try and get a grasp on things. "Right now, there should be more than a dozen pyramids all around the world releasing the anti-virus. According to the professor, they were connected, and this wouldn't have happened if they weren't all activated. It seems like it started working on Jake incredibly fast, but there's no way to know how long it'll take for everyone else. It might not even react the same way for someone who was completely changed. I'm hoping that it will at least buy the Khufu Bast some time, and maybe we'll be able to figure out how to help them."

Jake and Baxter come to sit with us and I'm starting to feel like we have been in one spot for too long. It would be a mistake to think that we're out of danger now.

"We don't even know who to trust," Chris presses, and I hate to admit that he's right. Taking his hand in mine, I have a strong feeling that our journey together is just beginning. I wrap my free arm around my little brother and he doesn't resist when I pull him even closer.

"We can trust each other," I say to them both, and we sit in silence for a minute, thinking back over everything that's happened.

A cracking branch reminds me that we are still too exposed. We all sit back, turning towards the sound. "There could be more Shiners out here," I whisper. "They wouldn't have just sent a few after us. Did you see any when I was gone?"

"We saw some movement nearby earlier, but they weren't interested in us," he answers, gathering the few items next to him into the backpack. "I think that all they cared about was finding and stopping you. Obviously, that didn't work out for them."

I can't help but smile, but then I grow serious again when I lift his shirt away from the wound on his side. It stopped bleeding, but it's ugly, and I'm afraid that as soon as he moves it'll start oozing again. Looking around somewhat helplessly, I try to come up with a plan. "We have to get you back to the cabin."

"Maybe we can help with that."

Jumping at the voice behind me, I spin around, my hand going automatically to the rifle slung over my back. Standing at the edge of the clearing, is our neighbor.

"Hey, it's Brent's dad!" Jake yells. I place a hand on his arm, just in case he was thinking about going to him. Baxter growls quietly, but remains at Jacob's side.

I don't know Brent's dad that well, but even I can tell that he looks confused and not confident like my mom and the others have been acting. His eyes are still glowing, but dimly. He rubs his hands together nervously and shifts from one foot to the other. Maybe the first thing that goes is the connection they all share, the single purpose that was driving them. I relax my grip on the rifle slightly.

"I don't understand what's going on," he continues, not moving any closer, "or why I'm in the woods. I want to get out of here and go home and find my family, but it's obvious that you need some help first, Alex." Gazing fearfully at the dark woods, he runs a hand through his hair in a very human gesture. My hopes rise.

There's movement behind him, and stepping out of the shadows and into the glow of the candlelight ... is my mom. Her blonde hair is loose and messy, framing her face the way she used to wear it. Not moving with the same grace and poise of a Shiner, she stumbles forward and looks quickly from Jake, to Chris, and then me. Praying again with my newly restored faith, I smile cautiously at her.

The forest grows still and then relief floods me as she smiles back. More important than the curve to her lips is the undeniable love that's shining in her normal, blue eyes. Encouraged, I kneel back down next to Chris as they make their way to us.

"Now what?" he asks me quietly, with guarded optimism.

"Now we go back and pick up what's left," I say with determination. "Then we wait." Looking up at the dark sky pierced by the still throbbing light, I wonder at what might be out there, coming for us. "If we have to ... we fight."

THE END

Alex's story continues in book two and three of the Forgotten Origins Trilogy: HERITAGE *and* DESCENT.

Available now at all major distributors!

ABOUT THE AUTHOR

Author Tara Ellis lives in a small town in beautiful Washington State in the Pacific Northwest. She enjoys the quiet lifestyle with her husband, two teenage kids and several dogs. Having been a firefighter/EMT and working in the medical field for many years, she now teaches CPR and concentrates on family, photography and writing young adult novels.

Visit her author page on Amazon to find all her books! http://www.amazon.com/author/taraellis

44629088R00149

Made in the USA
San Bernardino, CA
20 January 2017